Wild
Science

Amazing Encounters

Between Animals and the

People Who Study Them

Victoria Miles

RAINCOAST BOOKS

Vancouver

For Emily, may your heart lead
and your head follow.

Raincoast Books gratefully acknowledges the ongoing support of the Canada Council for the Arts; the British Columbia Arts Council; and the and the Government of Canada through Department of Canadian Heritage Book Publishing Industry Development Program (BPIDP).

Cover and interior design by Gabi Proctor/DesignGeist
Illustrations © Garth Buzzard
Photo credits on page 164

National Library of Canada Cataloguing in Publication

Miles, Victoria, 1966-
         Wild science : amazing encounters with animals and the people who study
them / Victoria Miles.

Includes index.
ISBN 1-55192-618-0

         1. Endangered species—North America—Juvenile literature. 2. Zoologists—North America—Juvenile literature. I. Title.

QL26.M54 2004   j591.68′097   C2003-906948-6

library of congress catalogue number: 2003116294

Raincoast Books   *In the United States:*
9050 Shaughnessy Street   Publishers Group West
Vancouver, British Columbia   1700 Fourth Street
Canada   V6P 6E5   Berkeley, California
www.raincoast.com   94710

At Raincoast Books we are committed to protecting the environment and to the responsible use of natural resources. We are acting on this commitment by working with suppliers and printers to phase out our use of paper produced from ancient forests. This book is one step towards this goal. It is printed on paper that is 50% recycled (30% post-consumer), elemental chlorine-and acid-free, and supplied by New Leaf Paper. It is printed with vegetable-based inks. For further information, visit our website at www.raincoast.com. We are working with Markets Initiative (www.oldgrowthfree.com) on this project.

Printed in Canada by Friesens

10 9 8 7 6 5 4 3 2 1

Contents

Foreword

When Chris and I travel the world on our personal mission to understand the amazing animals with whom we share this planet, we always end up running into one very fascinating species — the wildlife scientist. This animal is often found in remote regions living side by side with other wild species — and they have great stories to tell.

Indeed, a highlight of our creature adventures is sitting around campfires talking to like-minded wildlife scientists. Their stories can be funny, crazy or moving, but they always show the scientists' deep interest in animals, a commitment to understanding them, and a passion for their protection.

This book brings these scientists to people like you and me, people who love wildlife. It allows us to pull up a log around the fire and hear their stories. Plus, this book lets us hear the stories without logging thousands of miles to get to the scientists in the field. Although, I must warn you, after reading this book, you may find yourself compelled to head into the wilds and dedicate your life to learning just a little more about some incredible animal.

> Although, I must warn you, after reading this book, you may find yourself compelled to head into the wilds and dedicate your life to learning just a little more about some incredible animal.

See you on the creature trail,

Martin Kratt

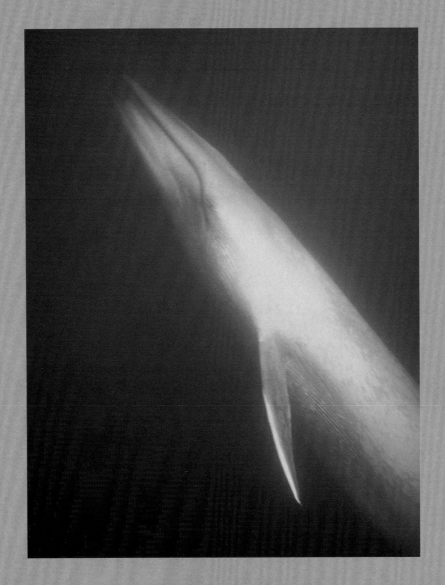

Nobody knew what kind of whale it was,
only that it was as big as a barn
and pale blue in colour.

Adult blue whales are the largest animals on earth.

FROM THE FIELD:

How to Save a Giant

The families of Brooklyn, Bonavista Bay, Newfoundland, had been watching the whale for weeks. They recognized it by the long white scars on its back — perhaps it had been struck by a ship, or caught in a fishing line. Every day the whale wandered up and down the fjord, as if it couldn't find its way back to sea. Everybody knew how murky and shallow the waters at the end of the fjords were. Dolphins and whales had stranded there before. Maybe the whale would figure its way out. Then again, maybe not.

One grey morning in September, everyone in the small fishing community awoke to see their worry come true. The whale had stranded. The tide was low and the whale's huge head and half its torso, as long as any of their homes, was up on the rocky shore. Nobody knew what kind of whale it was, only that it was as big as a barn and pale blue in colour.

A local fisheries officer made a phone call while families filed down to the beach to get a better look at the giant the tide had brought to shore. And then they all waited for the man who saves whales to arrive.

Around noon, a small pickup truck towing a zodiac poked down the narrow dirt road to the beach. When the doors opened two men stepped out: Jon Lien and his assistant for the day, Sean Todd, a graduate student at Memorial University of Newfoundland.

Immediately, a crowd gathered around the two men and anxious questions flew in the air. — What are you gonna do about the whale? Can you save it? Why's it here?

When everybody had calmed down a bit, Jon began to speak. He explained that strandings are a natural accident. They seem to happen most often to whales that are sick, old and confused with direction. Stranded whales are sometimes injured from being caught in fishing gear, or they might be quite young and malnourished. Sometimes they are badly infected by **parasites** or disease. No, Jon said, he wasn't sure yet if the whale could be saved. If a stranded whale was too sick, putting it back in the sea would just prolong its suffering. And even if it was still healthy, the community would have to be willing to help. First, Jon and Sean would have to do an examination. Then they would have more answers.

The men pulled on bright orange floater suits and began to rummage through

> Immediately, a crowd gathered around the two men and anxious questions flew in the air. "What are you gonna do about the whale?"

the truck for the right gear. Because most of the rescues Jon and his team perform are for whales trapped near shore in fishing nets, Jon's whale truck is always ready and packed with a lot of stuff you'd find in a fishing boat and some extras: rubber rain clothes, scuba gear and floater suits, a box of anchors and **grapnels**, sharp knives and gaffs (sticks with knives attached to the end), a block and tackle, lots of rope and pipes that can be screwed together to make a long arm to reach down into the water. The truck also carried a camera and scientific equipment including a tape recorder and an electrocardiograph (EKG) machine for measuring the whale's heartbeat. In case of an overnight job, the men had camping gear, a loaf of bread and a jar of peanut butter.

Identification was the easy part. Veterinarian Robert Hudson joined Jon and Sean to help make the examination. The giant's light blue, streamlined body, long pleated grooves on its underside, wide mouth covering baleen plates and barely noticeable dorsal fin near its tail were enough to confirm that this was, indeed, a blue whale.

Blues are not often seen in the waters around Newfoundland and Labrador. If they are spotted close to shore, it's usually in April or May and they are typically alone or with one or two others, feeding on swarms of krill. Their travels are carefully timed so they may enjoy two summers a year of the best krill-feeding in the rich "soup" of the polar seas. What this fellow was doing in Bonavista Bay in September was a mystery.

The whale measured about 14 metres (45 feet), about as long as a city bus. Knowing that adult blues can reach up to 27 metres (90 feet) in length, the scientists supposed he was probably quite young.

Despite the stranding, the whale seemed to be in good shape. A chunk of his dorsal fin was missing, but that had healed over; so had the scars on his back. He still had enough energy to roll and curl himself to keep his blowhole upright, his body did not appear to be infected by parasites and he smelled okay (whales with infected lungs tend to stink). Clouds overhead shielded his sensitive skin from sunburn. If the sun did come out, there was sunblock in the truck for rubbing over the whale's skin.

Jon ran his hand under the tail and found a vein, as wide as a pipe, pumping blood from a 182-kilogram (100-pound) heart. If the whale was dying, it likely would have shut down part of its circulatory system to reserve life-giving blood for those other vital organs, its brain and lungs. Using the EKG machine, the scientists recorded the whale's heartbeat. The heart was pumping steadily, if a bit fast, at 40 beats a minute. If the whale were diving, his heart would naturally slow to just a few beats a minute.

Sometimes, when Jon is working to cut a humpback whale out of a fishing net, he'll see fear and tension in the whale's eyes. "They'll do eye-catch with you," he says. "They look you in the eye. A frightened whale will stare back at you with big, wide eyes ringed by white." The big blue blinked and looked at Jon calmly from a dark eye the size of a grapefruit. He didn't seem particularly scared. Neither was Jon.

The tide was starting to rise by the time the men decided this strong young whale had a chance. But if they were going to attempt his rescue, they would have to start right away. If the whale was still here in a day or two it would die, crushed under the weight of its own body. Like two Lilliputians at work on a sleeping Gulliver, Jon and Sean snapped on their snorkels and waded into the water to tie ropes around the whale's **pectoral** fins and rig them into a makeshift bridle. The fisheries officer helped arrange to borrow a fishing boat from one of the local men. With the ends of the rope bridle securely hitched to the boat, the fisherman throttled the engine slowly forward, picked up the slack in the rope and pulled.

The whale didn't budge. The little boat pulled on. And on. Jon and Sean, up to their shoulders in the rising tide, pushed. The whale began to shift and struggle. That would help. With the boat still straining, the whale finally slid down the shore and into the sea. Right away, Jon and Sean unhooked their ropes from around the whale's flippers. Then they powered up their inflatable and, perched in it, began to dart from one side of the whale to the other, steering him in the right direction.

Using its pectoral fins to steer and its tail for power, the whale swam about 100 metres (328 feet) along the fjord and ... beached again!

Using its pectoral fins to steer and its tail for power, the whale swam about 100 metres (328 feet) along the fjord and ... beached again!

Scientists and fishers work to free a stranded whale.

Jon's stomach began to growl. Good thing he'd brought that peanut butter and bread: there'd be no hot meal at home tonight. The fishing boat returned and the whale was rigged up for a second tow. They got him off and heading in the right direction as before, but the whale was still confused. A few minutes later, he grounded again.

The men buckled down for a third try. This time the whale seemed to get the drift of what he was supposed to be doing. He began to head for the open sea. But just when things were going well, he detoured inland again toward a tiny harbour. He spooked two boys fishing on the dock before Jon zoomed up to him in the Zodiac, got him back on course and chased him out to sea.

Finally, far from land, the whale gradually began to get his bearings back. Jon and Sean hovered around him for a couple of hours to make sure he was okay. There would be a few rope burns around his flippers for a while, and part of his underside was scraped raw from the rocky shore, but Jon knew these marks would heal. Whales shed and replace their skins constantly.

It was about 9 p.m. when the Zodiac returned to the beach. A television crew was waiting. Jon was dead tired but he still wanted to talk to them about beached whales and blue whales. After the TV crew got their clip, Jon and Sean collected their equipment, put it back in the truck and set off for St. John's.

Over 20 years, Jon has rescued some 700 whales and other marine mammals. He says he's just a guy who "hangs out with a famous animal." His reward for the blue whale rescue? A dry change of clothes, a plain peanut butter sandwich and a really good night's sleep.

In a place where many fishers think of whales as net-damaging nuisances, people learned a little more from the rescuers about the mother of all giants, the blue whale. Later, whale researchers half a world away would marvel over the first electrocardiogram of the heartbeat of a blue whale. Of course, the big blue scored best — he got his life back. If you add it all up, everybody got something that day. That's how you save a whale.

THE SCIENTIST:

Jon Lien

D r. Jon Lien teaches in the biology and psychology departments of Memorial University of Newfoundland. For more than 25 years, his research has concentrated on how human activities, particularly inshore fishing, affect **cetaceans.**

Lien was born in Clark County, South Dakota — about as far from the ocean as anywhere you can be. "I grew up in a rural area," he says, "and from the time of primary school I was busy helping on a relative's farm and raising my own animals — chickens, rabbits, pigs. By the time I was in high school, I was raising flocks of 500 chickens several times a year, and buying calves each spring. I'd herd them in the ditches for free grass as a summer job, and sell them in the fall when school started. I always thought I would become a farmer. But a vet in my town talked me into going to university to become a vet and then come back and work in his practice. I was always bugging him with questions about sick animals, and he thought I had potential in that field. My parents were very religious but totally permissive with their kids. As they didn't have much schooling they were very proud of my work at university."

His education, beginning with a bachelor's degree at Minnesota's St. Olaf College through to his doctorate in science, focused on studies of animal behaviour. "I've always been fascinated with animals and how they work," he says. "From earliest memories I've considered them best friends. So at university and in graduate school it was natural to work in departments of psychology, zoology, animal sciences and at a **primate** research centre. My broad interest in animals eventually led me to become an animal behaviourist — a perfect job for me.

My work has enabled me to work with animals from sharks and squid to birds to **primates** and whales."

In his early efforts to find a solution to the problem of humpback whale entanglements in Newfoundland fishing nets, Jon first thought it would be easier to develop devices that would help whales detect and avoid the nets. What he's learned since is that understanding fishers is as important as understanding whales.

"I always thought I would become a farmer. But a vet in my town talked me into going to university to become a vet."

In their research to understand human attitudes toward whales, Jon and his associates learned that if you earn your living from the sea you're more inclined to think of a humpback whale as trouble. But working cooperatively with fishers to free a whale from fishing gear is in everyone's best interest. A live whale can be released more safely, quickly and with less costly net damage than a dead one can be cut loose. Over time, working with respected fishers (who could not only learn but also explain to other fishers the value of freeing whales while they were still alive) became one of the most valuable strategies of the Whale Research Group at Memorial University.

"I think the best advice for kids is to explore everything," Jon says. "Find what you like and then learn all you can about it. Best let your head follow your heart."

"Find what you like and then learn all you can about it. Best let your head follow your heart."

Jon Lien heads back for a hard-earned peanut butter sandwhich.

III THE SCIENCE:

Alarming Nets

Nobody really knows why whales strand. Strandings are a natural accident that can't be prevented. Most whale accidents, however, don't happen on the beach; they happen when whales become entrapped in fishing gear. Most of the whales caught in fishing gear are humpbacks (and of those the majority are juveniles, "the teenage drivers" of the seas), or "trouble" to the fishers whose nets they damage. The Whale Research Group offers entrapment assistance to help release trapped whales and to free fishing gear with the least amount of damage. While Jon and the group have become skilled in this sort of whale rescue, the work is dangerous, difficult, and still leaves nets in need of repair.

So while the group became better at freeing tangled whales, they were also developing a device to keep them out of nets in the first place. "You cannot change a whale's mind about where it wants to eat," says Jon. But you can discourage it from swimming into a fishing net — as long as the net is equipped with acoustic alarms.

Acoustic alarms are specially designed fishing floats that attach to fishing nets and beam out a steady, battery-operated clanging sound.

"Whale alarms work by simply making nets noisy," says Jon. The sound effect is like a bunch of New Year's party-goers banging on cooking pots with metal spoons: annoying but harmless. Partly because sound travels faster and four to five times farther in water than in air, whales can hear a net's alarms from up to 100 metres (328 feet) away. The sound alerts whales that there is something ahead of them, but does not harm their hearing.

The trick in designing the acoustic alarm was to get a "clang" that was near the peak of a whale's hearing sensitivity (in other words, unpleasant to listen to) but outside his frequency range, so as not to interfere with his **echolocation** or communication. People don't hear well under water, but whales do. Whales are so dependent upon their sense of hearing that it's been said, "a deaf whale is a dead whale." The sound also had to be set so that target fish species were not deterred from the direction of the net. "The fish weren't really the hard part," says Jon. "They tend to hear in the very low frequencies, whereas whales can hear a wider range of sound."

> Whales are so dependent upon their sense of hearing that it's been said "a deaf whale is a dead whale."

For Jon and his team, designing the alarm was a process of trial and error that paid off big time for whale conservation. Not only are alarmed nets a big, fat turnoff for whales, they've also been used effectively to discourage harbour porpoise net collisions. Today, many countries require **gillnetters** to use acoustic alarms in places where there is otherwise a high tendency for marine mammals to get caught accidentally in their nets.

THE ANIMAL NOTES:

Blue

Whale

Common name:	blue whale	**Suborder:**	Mysticeti (whales with baleen plates for food filtering, not teeth)	
Scientific name:	*Balaenoptera musculus*			
		Family:	Balaenidae	
Order:	Cetacea (mammals that live completely in water)	**Genus:**	*Balaenoptera*	
		Species:	*musculus*	

Protected from whaling since 1967, blue whales are slowly making a comeback; the oceans may be home to 10,000 of them today.

Size/weight:

Males can reach 26 metres (85 feet) and females 28 metres (90 feet). As heavy as a herd of elephants, a single blue can weigh up to 150 tonnes.

Description:

Their greyish blue skin is marked with light spots. They are streamlined with long, pleated grooves on the underside, a wide mouth and a small dorsal fin near the tail.

Reproduction:

Blue whales measure 7.5 metres (25 feet) long at birth and weigh seven tonnes.

Food:

Blue whales feed by straining "krill soup" through their 300 to 400 baleen plates. On a good day, blues can eat more than 3,200 kilograms (7,000 pounds) of krill (*Euphasia superba*).

Approximate lifespan:

Blue whales live about 80 years.

Status:

Before commercial whaling drove them to the edge of extinction, there may have been several hundred thousand blue whales worldwide. Protected from whaling since 1967, blue whales are slowly making a comeback; the oceans may be home to 10,000 of them today.

Habitat:

Blue whales migrate between temperate and subtropical zones to krill-rich polar seas in spring and summer.

Range/distribution:

Blues are found throughout the world's oceans.

FROM THE FIELD:

Emergence Day

The satellite image taken from space shows a flat mosaic of green forest and white snow.

On the ground, the picture is different. The place is known as the "Haley Bowl" and it's anything but flat: steep slopes, 1,300 metres (4,200 feet) high, snow-covered in April. Below is Haley Lake, a gem in the alpine landscape. Above are rocky outcrops that lead to Gemini Peak, and an avalanche bowl that spells danger for the unwary. Risk or no, studying Vancouver Island marmots means going where they live and Haley Lake is one of those places.

It was April 28, 1997, emergence day — the first day of the year that marmots tunnel through the snow from their underground **hibernacula**. Andrew Bryant made his way slowly and carefully across the slippery slope, the only way to move if he wanted to live to see the other side. With fewer than 100 animals left, the Vancouver Island marmot is one of the world's most endangered species. Because every marmot counts, Andrew could hardly wait for spring to find out who had made it from last year.

Nearing the other side, he was excited to see that a small opening, about 25 centimetres (10 inches) in diameter, had been tunnelled through the snow. When it comes to digging, says Andrew, marmots are like "little grizzlies." They have very strong back and shoulder muscles from a life of digging and tunnelling. With his spotting scope trained on the burrow entrance, Andrew patiently munched on cheese and crackers. He was just about to start in on a pepperoni stick when a small, chocolate brown head, led by a tiny black nose ringed in white fur and whiskers, poked out of the tunnel. Through his spotting scope, he made out the tag on the marmot's ear: number 97. *Well, for heaven's sake*, he thought to himself, *that's Bob Dole!*

With fewer than 100 animals left, the Vancouver Island marmot is one of the world's most endangered species.

How could he forget the first time he tagged number 97, a.k.a. Bob Dole! It was three years earlier, in the summer of 1994. Andrew was trapping and tagging marmots in Haley Lake Bowl with American marmot biologist Ken Armitage. Most marmots are pretty calm in traps, but number 97 was a real pain. He tried to bite Andrew, kept up a fierce scream-whistle all through the handling and was just plain grouchy about the whole process. It was Ken who suggested they call the marmot "Bob Dole," after the outspoken United States senator.

The same day Andrew caught Bob, he also caught number 254, a female. He decided to name her "Hillary," after the daughter of a friend.

Risk or no, studying Vancouver Island marmots means going where they live ...

Climbing Haley Bowl, part of Harley Lake Ecological Reserve, a protected area on Vancouver Island.

Now, almost three years after tagging Hillary and Bob, Andrew was embarking on another emergence day. Pumped and sweating from the climb, he reached for his Thermos and found himself shivering as he recalled a time a few years earlier when an emergence day much like this one turned into "emergency" day.

It happened on April 25, 1994. It began, as emergence day at Haley Bowl always did for Andrew, with an uphill ski along a snow-covered logging road leading toward the alpine forest of Gemini Peak.

His skis were fitted on the underside with skins, specially designed to grip the snow without slipping back. On his back, in an old grey pack, was 16 kilograms (35 pounds) of day gear: his ice axe, camera equipment, a field notebook, spotting scope, a Gore-Tex jacket in case the weather got nasty and lots of snacks. He also had safety gear and a first-aid kit.

Where the forest began Andrew stopped, took a swig of water from his canteen, rubbed the steam off the lenses of his sunglasses and took a good look around. He'd been skiing uphill for two hours. Sweat plastered his hair to his head and ran down the back of his neck. He was out of breath, his legs were shaky and the pack on his back cut into his sweaty shoulders. Other than that, he felt great. Really great.

The air was clear, the sky bright and sunny, and Andrew was surrounded by snow-covered mountaintops. The only other tracks in the snow around him were from cougars, squirrels, elk and deer. It was absolutely quiet. From somewhere over to his right, the still air carried the scratching of a brown creeper on a subalpine fir.

Swallowing one last gulp of water, he took off through the forest. In a couple of minutes he was through and out in the open, facing a steep, treeless avalanche bowl. Three hundred metres (985 feet) below, Haley Lake was still covered in ice. *Gee, it's sure a long way down.*

All he had to do now was cross to the other side where the marmots burrowed. Maybe he'd see Arnold. Or Meanie, who bit him in 1990. Or sweet little Runt.

Andrew removed his skis and took his ice axe out of his pack. He would use the axe like a handrail, planting it to anchor every step across the steep snowfield. Taking a deep breath, he began to move carefully across the slope. He knew that by late April there was little danger of avalanches. Still, he was cautious; danger lurked underfoot.

During winter, snowfall and temperature changes build up the snow in layers. Some layers may be hard and icy, and some soft and crumbly. Avalanches begin when snow layers separate and the top layers come sliding down. Here, avalanches can start in an instant, triggered by a skier or a bear or even a man with an ice axe.

Here, avalanches can start in an instant, triggered by a skier or a bear or even a man with an ice axe.

Andrew followed the best route over the bowl to avoid small slides. After every few steps he stopped and dug a hole in the snow to check out the layers. Step by step he neared the ridge from which he could spot the burrow entrance. *I wonder if Oprah survived the winter? That would make her nine years old, the oldest Vancouver Island marmot on record ...*

"SLOOSH!" The snow slipped out from under Andrew's foot. He was sliding downhill! In a second, he'd be caught in a torrent of snow and carried to the rocky outcrops below. He struggled and fought, swimming through the snow, and finally managed to throw himself off the slide. *Safe. Whoa ...*

Andrew's heart pounded in his throat as he watched the billowing slide race down the mountain. He knew he was lucky, that he could've gone down with it. Trembling from the scare, he looked over his shoulder and saw that the hibernation burrow was still snow-covered. The Haley Lake marmots weren't up yet.

The summit ridge was bare of snow and only 100 metres (28 feet) away. If he climbed straight up, sticking to the rocks, he could drop over the summit and check on the marmot colony on the other side at Bell Creek. Strapping the axe back on his pack, he stripped off his gloves and started up. He'd done it many times before, so

With fewer than 100 animals left, the Vancouver Island marmot is one of the world's most endangered species.

ABOVE: *Marmota, the marmot's scientific name, means "mountain mouse."*

RIGHT: *Every marmot counts! A tiny identification tag is attached to the marmot's ear so scientists can keep track of the population.*

he went straight for what climbers call a "jug" — the most solid, reliable handhold on a climb. This particular jug was a big piece of rock, about the size of a typewriter, that stuck straight out of the edge of the peak. Andrew knew he could grab it and swing himself right onto the peak — it was actually his favourite move on the whole route. It was dramatic and made it easy to pretend he was on Everest. He reached out with his right hand, grabbed the familiar shape and confidently put all his weight into the move.

Which is when the jug pulled loose.

The rock shook in his grasp. *Oh, no!* Andrew's mind reeled, thoughts of falling surging in on him.

Just as his left hand found a new grip and he began to steady himself, the jug broke free and smashed down on his right hand.

Yaaaaaaaaaaaaaaaaaagggggghhhhhhh!!! If the marmots had been awake they would have heard a strange sound — a very loud, pained, human scream.

Eventually, Andrew made it to the summit. There, at the top of the world, he cleaned and bandaged the gash on his hand.

That's when the cloud rolled in.

Man, this is not my day.

Thoughts of marmots were pushed aside as he started thinking about how he was going to get down the mountain.

A minute before, he had been sweating from the climb. Now he was sitting in a cloud, shivering from the cold and damp. Fortunately, there was an easier route down. Slowly, painfully, he began to descend, lowering himself into the most secure footholds. *Stay alert ... don't make a mistake ... no shortcuts ...*

It was nearly noon before he made it back to the forest to pick up his skis. Gliding through the stand of trees, Andrew started to feel a bit better. The cloud disappeared as he swished down the mountain to his truck. He told himself that it didn't matter if he didn't see marmots on this particular day: He had the whole summer ahead of him.

> But there are also those days when the mountain wins, and a researcher goes home with nothing new to add to the marmot notebook. Those are the days when it's just enough to get home safely.

When the weather is right and the marmots are out, Haley Lake can be a magical place. But there are also those days when the mountain wins, and a researcher goes home with nothing new to add to the marmot notebook. Those are the days when it's just enough to get home safely.

Andrew shook off the memory of this close call as he watched the now four-year-old Bob Dole leave the burrow. The marmot started sniffing around, searching for a patch where the snow had melted and he could nibble at the early grasses poking through. The meadow, slippery with dew, might be perilous, but it was ideal marmot habitat: steep and remote, with good soil for burrowing, boulders and rocks for lookout spots, and plenty of plants for food.

A movement caught the corner of Andrew's eye and he swivelled his scope back to the burrow entrance. *Well, whaddya know, Hillary's up! Now, wouldn't it be something if those two had pups?*

Three months later, the snow was gone and the Indian paintbrush was in bloom when a litter of four pups emerged from the burrow below Gemini Peak. Their parents? Hillary and Bob Dole.

II THE SCIENTIST:

Andrew Bryant

"I was one of those teenagers who couldn't quite decide whether I wanted to be a nuclear physicist or a fighter pilot," says Andrew Bryant. Born and raised in Quebec, he enjoyed camping and the outdoors as a teenager but "nothing in my background suggested I would ever develop a strong interest in biology."

When he was 19 he took a construction job in the Canadian Arctic. The stark beauty of the landscape and his first sighting of a polar bear got under his skin — and stayed. "So, never having taken a biology course in high school, I enrolled in an ecology program at the University of Waterloo. There I was introduced to statistics and report-writing, and a variety of other things that I couldn't quite see the point of. Then.

"In time, I met some excellent professors, including one who asked, 'Gee, I wonder why red-shouldered hawks are becoming so rare?' He challenged me to take this idea on as a research project. Two years later I'd handled a few birds, published my first scientific paper and learned more about the power of science to find solutions to real world problems. I was hooked on a path that would lead to butterflies and monkeys and owls and bears and, eventually, Vancouver Island marmots.

"Of all the important things I've learned about science, the single most valuable lesson is that it's okay to be wrong, and it's even better to learn from one's mistakes!"

Andrew is an independent conservation biologist based in Nanaimo, British Columbia. He earned a bachelor's degree in environmental studies from the University of Waterloo and a Master's in environmental design from the University of Calgary. He received his Ph.D. in biology from the University of Victoria in 1998.

"... the single most valuable lesson is that it's okay to be wrong, and it's even better to learn from one's mistakes!"

Independent conservation biologist Andrew Bryant and the marmot, Barbara.

III

THE SCIENCE:

Analysis of a Population Crash

The life history of marmots is impressive. Marmots use accumulated fat to fuel their bodies during winter, and they have a short summer in which to gain this fat and to breed. The average Vancouver Island marmot is active above ground for only five months of the year, and the harsh mountain climate means that the growing season is often much less than this.

Marmots can easily live 10 years and sometimes more, but often they don't begin to breed until they reach the age of three or four. They live in small colonies of fewer than half a dozen animals: typically a family group of mum, dad, a litter of three or four pups and a few subadults. These "teenage" marmots are interesting because some of them may disperse tens of kilometres to reach other colonies. The interchange of "new blood" among colonies is critical to survival of the whole population.

There have probably never been very many Vancouver Island marmots. Unlike the habitat of many other species of marmots, the natural meadows in which they live are few and far between. A curious feature of recent marmot history is the effect of forestry: During the 1980s, marmots expanded into new areas created by clearcut logging. In some years more marmots lived in such habitats than in natural meadows. Unfortunately, in recent years the total population has crashed in both natural and logged habitats. The last Haley Lake marmots died in 2000 and the species is now perilously close to extinction.

What's happening? Though many factors have contributed to this decline, some scientists believe that the reasons can be traced back more than 50 years to logging of the forests on Vancouver Island. Radio transmitters show that few marmots die in hibernation and most are killed by wolves, cougars and eagles. This is odd, because predators and marmots have co-existed for a long time. Something must have changed. It appears there is an unnaturally high level of predators and that the predators may be more successful at hunting marmots than they were before. After the forests were cleared, favourite deer foods such as alder grew back quickly and within a few years deer herds increased. This, in turn, meant more prey for wolves and cougars. And logging roads may have created easy travel corridors, "funnelling" predators into marmot habitat. The colonization of clearcuts by marmots themselves may have encouraged predators to spend more time there.

In the 1980s, deer populations began to decline. Meanwhile, the abnormally high predator numbers remained. Even an adult marmot in its prime isn't much bigger than a house cat, but for a hungry wolf or cougar it's definitely a healthy snack. From the late 1980s into the 1990s, marmot colonies and deer populations dwindled rapidly and evidence began to mount that an unsustainable level of predation on marmots was occurring.

It's hoped that forest regrowth will eventually restore a more natural balance of predators and their prey species, including marmots. However, this is a long-term proposition. In the short term it may be necessary to relocate or remove predators from marmot colonies, or to shepherd the marmots themselves.

Efforts to try to save the marmots have greatly intensified since late 1997, when a captive breeding program began and the not-for-profit Marmot Recovery Foundation was established. By 2002 the captive program had produced eight litters of pups. In the wild, field crews have moved marmots to other colonies to help "matchmake" by pairing lone marmots with eligible mates and this has also been successful. More marmots are scheduled for release in the future, offering real hope for a species bordering on extinction.

IV

Vancouver Island

28

Marmot

Common name:	Vancouver Island marmot	**Suborder:**	Sciurognathi
		Family:	Sciuridae
Scientific name:	*Marmota vancouverensis*	**Genus:**	*Marmota*
		Species:	*vancouverensis*
Order:	Rodentia		

The species is now perilously close to extinction.

Size/weight:

Marmots are the largest member of the squirrel family, almost as big as beavers. They typically weigh five to seven kilograms (11 to 15 pounds) and are heaviest in the fall, losing about one-third of their body weight over the winter hibernation.

Description:

The size of a large house cat, Vancouver Island marmots have rich chocolate brown fur and contrasting white patches around the black nose and on the chest. Marmots are very vocal and have different types of alarm calls, varying in pitch.

Reproduction:

Marmots live in colonies made up of (on average) fewer than five adults and a variable number of young — some yearlings, some two-year-olds and any pups born that year. Litters are usually three or four pups, born in late May or early June.

Food:

Vancouver Island marmots are highly selective feeders depending on time of year. They eat what plants are in season and available in their mountain meadow. Grasses and spreading phlox are very important marmot foods in the spring. As summer progresses they switch to lupines, asters, sweet peas and pearly everlasting. And, of course, the chunky peanut butter that researchers use in their traps.

Approximate lifespan:

Marmots can reach the age of ten, and sometimes up to twelve.

Status:

With a population containing fewer than 100 individuals, the Vancouver Island marmot is one of the world's most endangered species. Listed as endangered in 1980, populations have declined dramatically since then. Logging, climate changes, predators and disease have caused their numbers to decline close to extinction.

Habitat:

Marmots live in steep and remote meadows kept free of trees by avalanches, with good soil, boulders and rock and plenty of vegetation.

Range/Distribution:

Vancouver Island marmots live on Vancouver Island, British Columbia, Canada.

In the middle of this white desert a polar bear plodded from one spot to the next, the wind driving his body scent backward.

On the ice, sniffing the air to catch the scent of a seal.

From the Field:
Patience and the Polar Bear

All winter long, blistering Arctic winds packed down snow over the sea ice surrounding Radstock Bay on the south-west coast of Devon Island in the territory of Nunavut in northern Canada. Now it was the middle of April and snow, as deep as two metres (six and a half feet) in the pressure ridges and frozen as hard as concrete, covered most of the ice. In the middle of this white desert a polar bear plodded from one spot to the next, the wind driving his body scent backward. The bear walked this way on purpose—nothing in his path would smell him coming, while the wind delivered scents of what was ahead straight to his nose.

Sniffing the air, the bear slowed his gait and began to creep steadily on his broad, silent footpads toward another drift. He stopped and pointed his long, Roman nose down at the snowdrift. He had sniffed where a female ring seal had dug out a lair in an otherwise featureless drift. If he timed his next move right, he might eat today.

Two hundred metres (650 feet) above, at the top of a cliff known as Caswall Tower, Ian Stirling sat quietly inside an insulated plywood shack with his powerful telescope trained on the hunting bear. He couldn't see what was going on under the white crystal blanket, but he knew why the bear had stopped.

Over the winter, when the ice covers the sea, each ring seal around Radstock Bay maintains three or four breathing holes by scratching away at cracks in the ice with clawed flippers. "For seals, it's like swimming up a chimney to breathe," says Ian. "Seals have fairly strong breath. A few breath molecules lingering on the ice would be a very powerful clue to a bear that a seal had visited the hole within the last few minutes." If a hole smells promising to a polar bear, the bear will stand over it and wait for the chance to thrust its long neck down and haul up a seal coming to the surface for air.

By mid-April the ice is covered in wind-packed snow. Starting from one of its breathing holes in the ice, a pregnant ring seal digs a narrow tunnel in the hard snow above her and carves out a snug lair, about 50 to 70 centimetres (20 to 30 inches) high. In the lair she gives birth to a single pup. For six weeks the pup nurses on its mother's rich milk. At weaning time, when it's about a month and a half old, the pup may weigh 20 to 25 kilograms (40 to 50 pounds) and more than half its weight is fat. It's that fat for which polar bears are hunting.

The temperature outside was minus 25 degrees Celsius (77 degrees Fahrenheit). Drafts of cold wind rushed through the shack's sliding glass window where Ian balanced his telescope, but a small fuel-oil space heater fought them back. Ian and his two research technicians, biologists Dennis Andriashek and Wendy Calvert, were dressed in insulated pants, boots and heavy sweaters to stay warm enough to work. Ian's parka and windproof pants hung by the door. If he lost sight of the bears with his telescope, he could whip on his outwear and rush outside without losing precious observation time.

Cape Liddon — their home from the middle of April till the middle of May — was complete with a sleeping tent pitched about 20 metres (66 feet) behind the shack, an outhouse, and inside the shack, a small cookstove and the space heater. There was no shower; instead, the scientists took sponge baths inside. The team brought in food that keeps well in a cold climate — such as carrots, potatoes and apples — and bread, meat and bagels that could be frozen. They had enough for a month and, if they were lucky this trip, a helicopter might drop in on them with some fresh fruit and vegetables. Otherwise, they'd be defrosting every meal.

Ian has spent thousands of hours watching bears through his telescope from Caswall Tower.

For 45 minutes all was still through the lens of Ian's telescope. Suddenly, the bear rose up on its haunches to its full height and in one swift movement smashed down with its forelegs. All the strength of its 500-kilogram (1,100-pound) frame hammered down on the drift.

Nothing. The young seal had escaped into the sea. If the bear had checked with Ian in the first place, the scientist could have told him his chances of catching the seal were slim because "polar bears are successful in less than two percent of their kills." If the getting's good, a polar bear may eat every three or four days; if food is scarce, it might be two weeks between meals.

Ian has spent thousands of hours watching bears through his telescope from Caswall Tower. If the weather is bright and clear and bears are in view, he might sit in front of the scope for 12 to 16 hours, taking a break only to go to the outhouse or fix a little dinner. Because polar bears can nap, or be active, at any time of the day or night, and mid-May is the start of 24-hour daylight in the Arctic, the telescope is staffed round the clock.

The bears have no idea that Ian, Wendy and Dennis are watching them, but seabirds — gulls, kittiwakes and fulmars — know of the people on the cliff. About 50,000 fulmars flock to the cliff to breed each year, and some of them show special interest in the camp. They float on the strong winds funnelling up the cliffside and hover a metre or two (3 to 6 feet) outside the shack, looking through the window at the scientists inside.

Fog is another regular visitor to the cliff and may stay for two or three days at a time. "We're either in the fog, or above it," says Ian. "Down at ice level, under the fog, the bears can see and hunt just fine, but we lose track of them." The scientists use the time to catch up on their sleep, take sponge baths, fix up their field notes and take a little more time to prepare better meals.

If a hole smells promising to a polar bear, it will stand over it and wait for the chance to haul up a seal coming to the surface for air.

ABOVE: *Scientists at Cape Liddon record information on a tranquilized bear.*

LEFT: *The camp at Cape Liddon. Scientists sleep in the tent and work in the cabin.*

From his sea-cliff perch, Ian has learned that polar bears have a general rule of "not doing anything quickly." With their thick fur, tough skin and blubber layer, polar bears live comfortably in the cold. If they exert too much energy they run the risk of overheating. Still, they can move quickly when it's necessary.

A few days later, Ian was at the window watching another polar bear in action. This time he had his telescope focused on a "very, very large male" with a female in his company. While April and May are two of the best months to watch polar bears hunt, they are also mating months for the bears.

> **With their thick fur, tough skin and blubber layer, polar bears live comfortably in the cold.**

As Ian watched, a challenger male with long, black scars came into sight. Under its white coat, a polar bear's skin is black. When a bear is wounded the cut heals over, but fur does not grow back over the scar. This newcomer was obviously an experienced fighter and a battle over the female was about to break out on the ice. Ian had seen bears fight for mating rights plenty of times before. He knew that scraps could last well over a half hour, so he settled down to watch the fight unfold.

But the big, dominant male had a surprise in store. He took a lunging rush at the intruder, grabbed his neck in his jaws, flipped him over and pinned him to the ice. He stood there, his teeth wrapped around the throat of his challenger, for 10 or 20 seconds. "He took just enough time to show who was boss, then he let him go," says Ian. A couple of days later a second bear, as scarred with experience as the first, "got thumped just as quickly." Ian's never seen such a fast fight. "Clearly," he says, "this dominant male was at the top of the heap."

Even though there is plenty of physical competition between male bears to decide who will win a female to mate with, usually polar bears are excellent at conserving energy. "They are a lot like misers that hate to part with their money," says

Ian. "They don't use energy for anything unless they absolutely have to." Still, just because a polar bear is lying down doesn't mean it's napping. Oftentimes, they lie in wait for the snout of a seal to pop up through a breathing hole. They may wait without moving a centimetre for 45 minutes or more for a chance to haul a seal out of the ice. Though an average wait is 45 minutes, they can stand for several hours in one place. Polar bear scientists call this method "still-hunting," and they have found that most of the time this waiting game is the way polar bears catch their seals.

By the time the researcher's month is up Ian will have spent hundreds of hours at the window, watching the polar bears of Radstock Bay. He's always glad to spend a month at Caswall Tower "letting the animals tell their own story." More than anything else, he thinks his time spent patiently at the telescope has helped him to understand what it means to be a polar bear.

THE SCIENTIST:

Ian Stirling

D r. Ian Stirling is a senior research scientist for the Canadian Wildlife Service and an adjunct professor of zoology at the University of Alberta. He is considered to be a world expert on polar bears and their role in Arctic ecosystems.

Ian says it is a "privilege to be able to sit in a totally wild place, see the weather change and watch polar bears." But one of the things he's seen emerge is evidence that the polar bears of Hudson Bay, which he also studies, are getting thinner. In fact, they are about 10 percent thinner than they were 20 years ago. Meanwhile, the ice they depend on for hunting seals and mating is thinning, too. For scientists who know the Arctic, the correlation between global warming, shrinking ice, and thinner bears is getting clearer with every centimetre that melts away. "We can understand the effects of the climate changes that are taking place in a polar environment by studying its resident polar bears and seals," says Ian. "Like all animals at the top of the food chain, the health and the state of their populations is a very good indicator of the state of their environment."

Ian has been observing connections between ecosystems and wildlife for most of his life. He grew up in a small mining town in southeastern British Columbia where his family enjoyed the outdoor life — everything from camping and hiking to fishing, hunting and birdwatching. And he had another pastime: collecting. Birds' nests, bones, animal skulls, antlers, they all were hauled into the Stirling household. "My mother was extremely tolerant of everything I dragged into the house," he says.

There was a scientist in the family, a geologist uncle who worked in Africa but visited periodically and talked to Ian about science and his work. And a couple of

Ian says it is a "privilege to be able to sit in a totally wild place, see the weather change and watch polar bears."

Ian Stirling befriends a young polar bear cub.

Ian has been observing connections between ecosystems and wildlife for most of his life.

Ian's father's friends were hunters who let him go along on some of their trips. "These men had vast stores of knowledge about wildlife," Ian remembers. "They loved to be out in nature and they had a strong conservation ethic — by that I mean they hunted within sustainable limits, even though nobody called it 'sustainable limits' in those days. They just knew not to take too much, not to take more than what nature could restore."

As he grew older, Ian took to exploring the mountain surroundings of his hometown on skis. He became adept at observing seasons and conditions and their effects on wildlife. "My first thought of a career was that I might grow up to be a game warden. It was while I was looking into that kind of work that I learned about wildlife biology. And the more I found out, the more that sounded like what I wanted to do with my life."

THE SCIENCE:

Observing Polar Bears

The zoom telescope Ian Stirling uses to watch polar bears at Radstock Bay has a magnification range of 15 to 60 times; usually, Ian works with it magnifying bears' images by about 20 or 25 times.

In spring and summer, there is 24-hour daylight on Devon Island. The scientists sleep in short shifts and take turns at the telescope 24 hours a day, seven days a week.

The fact that there are no trees on Devon Island to block the view is ideal for telescopic observation in good weather. But when fog or a storm rolls in, it can sock in Cape Liddon and act as a curtain between the scientists and the bears. The fog can stay for days, however, making the telescope about as useful as a TV with no cable.

Not all the work is indoors. The bears are tagged and tracked for information about their movement and survival. Ian has crawled into polar bear dens and ID-tagged, tattooed and radio-collared tranquilized bears to track them by satellite **telemetry**.

Even studies of polar bears in captivity are enlightening. For example, feeding tests on captive polar bears have shown that they can switch their **metabolic** rate down if food disappears, to help them conserve energy and prevent starvation — a kind of "walking hibernation."

"All these methods are important for helping us understand things such as polar bear movement patterns and survival or reproductive rates," Ian says, "but to learn how they live in their habitat on a day-to-day basis, direct observation is one of the most interesting."

THE ANIMAL NOTES:

Polar

Bear

Common name:	polar bear	Family:	Ursidae
Scientific name:	*Ursus maritimus*	Genus:	*Ursus*
Order:	Carnivora	Species:	*maritimus*
Suborder:	Fissipedia		

Global warming is now perhaps the greatest threat to polar bears, since they depend upon their sea ice habitat to catch seals.

Size/Weight:

Full-grown males typically weigh between 350 and 650 kilograms (770 and 1,500 pounds). Adult females are between 150 and 250 kilograms (330 and 550 pounds) although a pregnant female may be as large as 500 kilograms (1,100 pounds). Polar bear cubs weigh about 0.6 kilograms (1.3 pounds) at birth and in their first two years (if they survive) will grow to be almost as big as their mothers.

Description:

The polar bear has white fur, while its nose, lips and eyes are black. A polar bear's skin under the fur is also black. It has thick fur, tough skin and a blubber layer that keeps it warm.

Reproduction:

April and May are the mating months for polar bears. Males challenge each other for mating rights with females. Litters of one to four cubs are born around November–January in a winter den. On average a female has a litter only every three years. When cubs are born they are vulnerable to many dangers. They remain with their mother for about a year and a half, denning with her the winter after their birth, but still only about six out of every 10 cubs make it through the first year of life. Starvation, predation by male polar bears and accidents take the rest.

Food:

The polar bear is the most carnivorous bear in North America. Seals are its main food — a polar bear will wait at a seal's breathing hole in the ice without moving, often for hours. Polar bears also eat fish, birds, birds' eggs, small mammals and dead animals. Fat is important to its diet, so much so that it will not spend its own energy to eat a scrawny seal pup. A successful polar bear may eat every three or four days; if food is scarce it might go two weeks between meals.

Approximate lifespan:

Male polar bears commonly live up to about 25 years of age. Females often live into their late twenties.

Status:

In the 1960s overhunting of polar bears was a serious concern. They are now protected by agreements signed by all countries where polar bears are found: Canada, the United States, Greenland, Norway and Russia. The hunting of polar bears is reserved for Native peoples. Scientists estimate there might be anywhere from 20,000 to 25,000 polar bears worldwide. About 15,000 of those live in Canada. For now this is considered a fairly healthy number, but polar bears are vulnerable to environmental catastrophes, such as oil spills, and they can still be killed legally if they pose a danger to humans. Pollution, even that which originates in faraway places, is another threat to Arctic life and scientists have been discovering higher and higher levels of contaminants in polar bears. Global warming is now perhaps the greatest threat to polar bears, since they depend upon their sea ice habitat to catch seals. If the Arctic were to warm by even three or four degrees more, it could have serious consequences for polar bears.

Habitat:

Polar bears are found throughout the ice-covered waters of the Arctic region and prefer to remain out on the sea ice all year if possible. As the ice retreats north during the summer months, polar bears travel with the ice floes.

Range:

Polar bears are usually found in the northern marine areas of the state of Alaska, Norway's Svalbard Archipelago, Russia, Greenland and Canada.

Marianne was just about to call it quits when two tiny paws landed on her shoulders.

Watching his substitute mom, the orphaned sea otter pup learns how to open the hard-shelled prey they have found.

Swimming
with Sea Otters

I

It was no use. She couldn't do it. Marianne Riedman was trying to dive 10 metres (30 feet) to the bottom of the kelp forest, find something a sea otter would eat, and surface with it before she ran out of air. She'd been in the cold water of Monterey Bay for 45 minutes, had made 25 dives and almost every time, had come up with nothing.

Marianne's teeth started to chatter. She couldn't stay out much longer. She was just about to call it quits when two tiny paws landed on her shoulders.

The paws belonged to Pico, the orphaned sea otter pup she was supposed to be teaching to **forage**. Pico climbed onto her head and crouched, clinging to her hood. From there he peered back at the other sea otters rafting nearby in the kelp forest canopy.

It's not easy to be a sea otter mother, thought Marianne as the water from Pico's fur trickled down her mask.

Under water, some prey stayed hidden from her and some were just plain hard to see, but in an hour Marianne could usually find some small stuff. What was difficult was finding enough food for a hungry otter pup.

Sea snails were easy: she could pick those right off the kelp **fronds.** But snails are difficult to open and Pico didn't seem to like them, anyway. If she found an abalone, she couldn't pull it off its hold. Abalone have a really tight grip and even a wild, wave-whipping storm can't loosen them. Once in a while Marianne would spot a big cancer crab poking its way around a kelp **holdfast.** They were hard to handle but Pico always ate them, so Marianne figured they were worth the risk of getting pinched through her gloves. Sometimes she might find a sea urchin. She knew how to pick those off the ocean floor and crack them open by their underside, where no prickly spines grew.

> **She was supposed to be imitating a real otter mother, and real otter mothers don't wear oxygen tanks on their backs.**

If Marianne could use a scuba tank she'd have more time under water to gather prey. But she was supposed to be imitating a real otter mother, and real otter mothers don't wear oxygen tanks on their backs. They make short dives, no more than about four minutes each, then surface. If they are successful they bring up something to eat in their paws or pocketed in one of the flaps of skin hidden next to either arm.

Marianne couldn't hold her breath for four minutes. One minute was her max.

Tomorrow I'm bringing out a goody bag full of rock crabs, she thought. Pico could watch her dive and bring them up for cracking. As long as there were no other otters around who might be tempted to steal Pico's snacks, Marianne could get away with it. It was cheating to bring up so many at a time, but Pico wouldn't get enough to eat if her "mom" kept coming up empty-handed.

Marianne was just about to head for the shore when she was stopped by a sharp banging sound.

"Clack! Clack! Clack!" She turned to face the direction from which the sound was coming. A female sea otter was banging a crab on a flat rock she'd balanced on her chest. She was so close that Marianne recognized her as a small female who had been studying them for the past couple of days. Most sea otters are wary of humans but this one was always very calm, almost friendly, when Marianne and Pico were around. She treated Marianne as if she was another otter and sometimes swam up to nudge and nuzzle her with her nose.

Marianne watched the little creature tear pieces of crabmeat out of the shell and noisily chew away, making loud, smacking sounds as she mashed each bite in her mouth.

The otter finished her meal, swept the rock and shell pieces off her chest and somersaulted in the water to rinse the oil and crab bits off her fur. After a quick scrub, she dived again. In a split second Marianne decided to go after her. Where she dived, Pico would follow. They both might have something to learn from the female otter, who looked well- fed and healthy.

In a few seconds, all three were at the bottom of the kelp forest. This time Marianne didn't bother trying to find anything by herself — she just watched the female. And what she saw intrigued her.

With her tiny forepaws the otter pushed and pulled at boulders on the substrate. Once she'd rolled them out of the way, she could easily get at the crabs hiding underneath. Until that moment, Marianne had thought that otters mostly patted along the bottom to find food and relied on their eyesight and sensitive whiskers for more foraging clues. This otter was showing her a totally different technique.

It's not easy to be a sea otter mother, thought Marianne as the water from Pico's fur trickled down her mask.

An orphaned sea otter pup in training may have a chance at life in the wild.

Marianne looked around for a rock of her own. There were plenty to choose from and, sure enough, the first stone she turned had a startled crab underneath. She picked it up and kicked her fins to rise.

At the surface, she gasped for breath. She couldn't have stayed down a second longer, but it didn't matter — she'd learned what she needed to know. Even better, Pico had seen it, too. Within a couple of minutes he was scarfing down a crab caught by his very own substitute mother.

Pico was named for Pico Creek, in southern California, where he was found on June 26, 1988. He was only two weeks old when he was orphaned and no one knows what happened to his mother. Orphaned pups less than four months old have a very poor chance of survival and they sometimes wash up on California beaches starved, injured or drowned. Fortunately for Pico, the people who found him acted quickly. He was rushed to the Monterey Bay Aquarium where a team of people, including Marianne, was ready to step in and try to substitute for his missing mom.

The work to care for an orphaned pup was constant. In the first month of his stay at the aquarium Pico was looked after by a steady stream of biologists and volunteer otter-sitters. They fed him a milkshake formula of clams, squid, fish oil, dairy cream, fluids, vitamins and minerals. They cleaned, dried, combed and brushed his fur to keep it fluffy. They even played with him and gave him rubber toys to chew and dunk in his saltwater tank.

Pico couldn't stay at the aquarium forever — its sea otter exhibit was already home to four otters who couldn't survive on their own in the wild. But he had a pretty good chance to learn how to fend for himself in the kelp forests of Monterey Bay, even though when his mother disappeared he lost his best teacher of survival skills. She would have shown him where to find spiny sea urchins, pinching crabs or stubborn abalone at the bottom of the kelp forest. If he watched her carefully he would have learned how she used her jaws, paws, rocks and other tools to open her hard-shelled prey. Now he would have to have humans try to teach him how to forage for food — his other survival skills would come naturally. The aquarium gave him several substitute moms to make up for the one he'd lost and one of them was Marianne.

When Pico was six weeks old he started daily swimming lessons with Marianne in the aquarium's outdoor tide pool. In the beginning, she tried to get his attention by cracking open crab and urchin shells and feeding him bites. But Pico wasn't interested — he wanted to play. Although his extra-buoyant baby fur gave him his own built-in life jacket, it made it difficult for him to dive. When he tried to follow Marianne under water, he popped back up like a bobbing bathtub toy.

> **He was bigger, stronger and ready to start foraging lessons in the kelp forests of Monterey Bay.**

By the time he was about three months old, Pico's thick adult fur had grown in. He was bigger, stronger and ready to start foraging lessons in the kelp forests of Monterey Bay.

After the day when the little female otter let Marianne in on her food-finding secret, Pico began to copy what Marianne was doing on their dives. He still played around a lot, grabbing her hood and hanging onto her fins for a ride, but it wasn't long before he was finding a little food for himself between bouts of goofing off.

Like all young otters, Pico made mistakes. Pups pick up a lot of junk on the kelp forest floor before they figure out what's food and what isn't. Young otters learn by trial and error that pieces of wood, empty shells and pine cones are not food. Where there are careless humans nearby, otters also find cans, bottles, plastic bags, drinking straws and old shoes where they're foraging. But through all his mistakes and his successes, Pico learned.

On February 14, 1989, when he was about eight months old, his swimming and foraging lessons came to an end. He was released on his own into the tidal basin at the aquarium. He had identification tags on both flippers and a radio transmitter implanted under the skin near his belly.

Eventually, he turned up in the waters north of Santa Cruz, a popular spot for young male sea otters. For many months researchers reported seeing him and they kept track of him with signals from his radio transmitter.

In September 1989, the signals stopped coming in.

It's possible that Pico moved out of the receiver's range, or that the batteries in his transmitter stopped working. He might have died, or simply lost his tags and joined the ranks of unidentified otters. The place where he was last seen is difficult to observe from shore. No one can say for sure how long he lived.

Whatever happened, in the months before he disappeared a healthy-looking, well-fed Pico was often seen feeding quite expertly on rock crabs — the same food Marianne had shown him how to find.

II

THE SCIENTIST:
Marianne Riedman

"I grew up in Long Beach, California, on the ocean," says Marianne Riedman. "We had a house on the bay, so naturally that made it easy to get in and on the water whenever I wanted. I was always pulling up some marine creature from our dock and examining it before letting it go.

"My Dad taught me to skin dive when I was seven, and I'll never forget the first time I put on a mask and snorkel and looked under water — it was incredible! We were at Catalina Island and I could see garibaldi fish and all sorts of marine life in the crystal clear water. We had a boat and would make the 40-minute trip to Catalina all the time. When I was 13, my dad taught my brother and I to scuba dive and that opened up a whole new world of exploring under water."

During Marianne's senior year in high school, Konrad Lorenz and Nikko Tinbergen won the Nobel Prize in science for their pioneering work in animal behaviour. "When I read about their work, I decided that this was the field I wanted to work in, so in college I majored in biology, with an emphasis on evolutionary biology and behaviour."

As an undergrad at the University of California at Santa Cruz, she became involved in several field studies, especially with the northern elephant seals that bred on an island north of Santa Cruz.

By the time she obtained her Ph.D. in biology, Marianne had been part of studies of sea turtles in Australia, Guadalupe fur seals off the coast of Mexico and marine

"I was always pulling up some marine creature from our dock and examining it before letting it go."

Marianne Riedman holds an orphaned sea otter pup.

> Marianne grew up to become not only a biologist but also the author of several books.

invertebrates, seals and sea otters along the coast of California. She specialized in the behaviour of marine mammals, sea otters in particular, and in 1985 she became director of sea otter research at the Monterey Bay Aquarium. Over the next 10 years her work with otters through the aquarium introduced her to many orphaned pups, including Pico.

It was Marianne's mother who instilled in her a lifelong love of books and writing. Marianne grew up to become not only a biologist but also the author of several books, including *The Adventures of Phokey the Sea Otter,* a children's picture book.

Some of the credit for her two careers goes to her parents, the rest to her for following what holds her interests and not letting go. As a teenager she tried working in a veterinarian's office one summer, but she didn't like the work as much as she'd hoped. For her, the fantasy of a veterinary career didn't quite measure up to its reality.

Marianne's advice comes straight from her own experience. "If you have a passion and love for the work, you will succeed at it no matter what. Find an adult who is doing exactly the kind of work you love, talk to them and volunteer to help. This is the best way to get valuable experience and find out what it's really like to work in their field."

THE SCIENCE:

Learning from
Compassion

arianne Riedman is the first to say that reintegrating an orphan sea otter pup into the wild is a "program of compassion."

"Most of the really good otter data come from observing wild otter behaviour, but as a field biologist it was a great chance to have such a close-up look into their world," she says of helping Pico. Most field biology is done at a distance; diving with otter pups gave her a chance to see their behaviour under water.

Michelle Staedler, who now manages the sea otter research programs for the Monterey Bay Aquarium, agrees with Marianne. "In the beginning, we didn't even know how to keep stranded otters alive," she says, thinking back to the early 1980s. "The very first otter rehab 'programs' were people putting injured otters in bathtubs so they wouldn't die." Today, the aquarium continues in its mission to inspire conservation in the oceans. Its "program of compassion" has given back a much deeper understanding of sea otter nutrition, **metabolism**, growth and development. Not only are stranded, ill or injured otters restored to health and successfully released back into the wild, but the aquarium is also now taking the sea otter program one step farther — its focus is now on discovering why California sea otters are threatened and how it can help the population thrive.

Every otter released from rehab at the aquarium leaves with a little more than it came in with. Tags like the one Pico had are no longer used, because they tend to fall off or get worked off by the otter. Instead, an otter is injected with a tiny transponder chip, under the skin of the groin area, which contains a unique code in case it is found or turns up stranded on a beach. Scientists check by running a scanning device over the area to read the chip and, if there is one, they match the data with their records and update the next or sometimes final chapter in the otter's life history.

An Otter may also be fitted with a radio transmitter implanted in the abdomen. If it is attached anywhere outside the body, the otter they could twist the loose skin around and get at it. In the surgery to fit the transmitter, a veterinarian makes a six-centimetre (two-and-a-half-inch) incision for the device, which is a little smaller than a deck of cards. Most of the 20-minute procedure is spent on the four layers of sutures needed to seal the wound. Afterward, the otter spends another two weeks under constant care and 24-hour camera surveillance to make sure nothing goes wrong before it is released back in to the wild. Some 70 otters have had the procedure and they've all come through it fine.

> She was supposed to be imitating a real otter mother, and real otter mothers don't wear oxygen tanks on their backs.

"When it comes to surgery, otters are incredibly resilient," says Michelle. "They are tough. We see them sometimes with broken flippers, or wounds that haven't healed, or shotgun pellets embedded in their skin. One otter had a pellet in his shoulder and no movement in his arm but he was still out there, still foraging with one arm."

In the first week after an otter's release, the radio transmissions help scientists follow the otter's progress in finding food and staying healthy. Some otters struggle after release, not feeding or finding food, swimming too far offshore, and so the researchers may have to go out and fetch them back to the aquarium to fatten up before they are re-released. Sometimes it takes several tries, and there are the rare otters that just don't get it, even after seven or eight go-rounds. Eventually, there comes a point when the otter is left to its own devices. "That's hard," says Michelle. "You don't want to see anything bad happen to them, but it's a wild animal and eventually you have to let it go."

As time goes by, otters toting tracking devices contribute valuable data on otter migration patterns and home ranges. A few of the study otters have travelled distances of more than 480 kilometres (almost 300 miles). The juveniles tend to travel more than the adults, but it's still hard to say why. Prey abundance, or searching for a particular kind of prey they like, may explain some of the places they choose, but they've also turned up in habitats where it's hard for an otter to make a living.

Tracking otters by radio telemetry from a small plane offers biologists a chance to observe unobtrusively not just where otters go, but what they do. It gives them glimpses into the world of nature that few people ever see.

THE ANIMAL NOTES:

Sea

Otter

Common name:	California sea otter, Alaskan sea otter	Suborder:	Fissipedia
		Family:	Mustelidae
Scientific name:	California sea otter: *Enhydra lutris nereis*	Genus:	*Enhydra*
		Species:	*lutris*
Order:	Carnivora	Sub Species:	*nereis*

Sea otters were once a common marine mammal throughout the coastal waters of the North Pacific. Today, California sea otters are found only in small numbers along the coast of California.

Size/weight:

Generally sea otter females may reach 1.4 metres (46 inches) and weigh 16 to 27 kilograms (35 to 60 pounds). Males grow up to 1.48 metres (4.9 feet) and weigh 27 to 39 kilograms (60 – 85 pounds). California sea otters average about 1.2 metres (4 feet) in length, while the Alaskan sea otter is slightly larger. Weights can vary depending on location and availability of food.

Description:

Sea otters have dark brown fur on their bodies with lighter, blondish fur on their heads. They have large, blunt teeth, small eyes and ears and webbed hind feet.

Reproduction:

Mother sea otters do all the pup-rearing. Usually, mothers have only one pup at a time, but occasionally a female will have twins. If this happens, she will abandon one of them because the work to feed, groom and protect herself and one pup is very difficult — raising two at a time is impossible.

Food:

Sea otters are intrepid foragers of marine invertebrates such as sea snails, abalone, crabs and sea urchins. They find food in short dives and bring it to the surface in their paws or pocketed in one of the flaps of skin hidden next to either arm. An otter will often balance a rock on its chest to break open shells.

Approximate lifespan:

Male sea otters live for 10 to 15 years, females for 15 to 20.

Status:

Sea otters were once a relatively common marine mammal throughout the coastal waters of the North Pacific. Today, California sea otters are found only in small numbers along the coast of California. Officially, they are a threatened species. By the early 1900s the California sea otter, Alaskan sea otter, *Enhydra lutris kenyoni*, and Russian sea otter, *Enhydra lutris lutris*, were virtually exterminated by overhunting for the fur trade. Today, California sea otters are protected animals and are slowly making a comeback in parts of their former range.

Habitat:

Sea otters are found near the shore in shallow waters. Kelp beds are an ideal environment for otters' preferred food.

Range/Distribution:

Sea otters range from central California north to Alaska, and westward along the Aleutian, Commander and Kuril Islands. They can also be found on the southern tip of Siberia's Kamchatka Peninsula and the southeastern coast of Sakhalin Island.

Research biologist Amy Robison leaped to her feet. "There's a manatee in distress down in the Trout River."

Manatees use their big, strong lips pads to tear off the tough stems and leaves of the plants they eat.

FROM THE FIELD:

Half-Moon Manatee

"**D**uval County Manatee Hotline, this is Amy speaking."

"There's a manatee in the river right down in front of my house," came a woman's worried voice from the other end of the line. "It's been here since dawn, sort of twistin' and rollin' around. You gotta get somebody out here — I think it's dyin'!"

Research biologist Amy Robison leaped to her feet. She noted the woman's address and a few more details and promised they'd be out right away. As soon as she'd hung up the phone, she raced down to the office where her boss, professor Quinton White, was getting his notes ready for his next lecture. Amy had worked with Quinton between 1993 and 2000, the first year the Jackson University Manatee Research Project began.

"Quint! There's a manatee in distress down in the Trout River," Amy blurted out. "Gerry's bringing the truck around, can you call Billy?"

Billy Brooks is a biologist at the Florida Department of Environmental Protection in Duva I County. He is responsible for manatee conservation in northeast Florida. If the manatee really was injured, there was only a slim chance it could be rescued. Wounded manatees are very skittish and difficult to catch. Usually, it's impossible for people to do anything for them. Billy would have to see this one and decide whether or not to call in a rescue team.

But it was possible this one wasn't injured. Quinton had a theory that might explain why the manatee was there: manatee cows are known to travel into the tributaries to give birth. In other parts of the world where manatees can be found, people have seen calves being born in safe, secluded waterways, far from rough, open seas and boats on busy rivers. The thing was, in Florida, no biologist had ever seen a manatee calf being born in the wild.

Out in the Jacksonville University parking lot, Gerry Pinto was waiting for Amy behind the wheel of one of the university's trucks. He'd been working on the manatee project for only a few months, but he had a feeling something big was about to happen. The manatee hotline hardly ever rang in April, because there were only a few manatees around. Most of them spent the winter further south in Blue Spring and were only now starting to come north for the summer. Gerry started the engine when he saw Amy running toward him and he leaned over to open the passenger door for her. She tossed the video camera on the seat beside him, jumped in and yanked the door shut. Gerry put his foot on the gas.

It took them about 20 minutes to get to the Trout River. They drove past farms and fisher's houses until they came to the address the woman had given Amy over the phone. "This must be it," said Amy. "Look, Billy's truck is here."

Water is everywhere in Jacksonville. It snakes through neighbourhoods, and

She looked like a gigantic grey potato
floating in rich, brown soup.
Amy guessed she weighed about
900 kilograms (2,000 pounds).

*Manatees live in turbid water and only surface to breath with the tip of their
snout showing above the water.*

people who live along the riverbanks sometimes spot the back of a cruising manatee from their living room windows. The woman's house fronted a quiet place on the river. It was no longer a popular spot for fishing: The water had silted in so much that Trout River was practically a lagoon.

Manatees can stay underwater for up to 12 minutes

The woman was waiting for them with Billy. She told them she'd lived on the river all her life, 60-some years. On this morning, she'd been sitting outside in her chair just "watchin' the river" when the manatee appeared. "There he is." The woman pointed a wrinkled, sun-browned finger down to the riverbank.

At first, all they could see was a pair of wide nostrils emerge and open for air. Then gradually the manatee's long, wide, grey back appeared and its tail broke the waterline.

Amy was dumbfounded. She'd seen three-metre-long manatees, but this one had to be at least 3.66 metres (12 feet). Female manatees are usually larger than males, so this was no "he" manatee, it had to be a "she." And the barrel around her middle! She looked like a gigantic grey potato floating in rich, brown soup. Amy guessed she weighed about 900 kilograms (2,000 pounds).

A dense border of thick marsh grass kept everyone back from the riverbank. Standing about 20 metres (65 feet) away from the manatee, the four people watched as she arched her back above the brackish water. They could hear her thrashing as she reversed the arch, dropped her belly low and held her nostrils and tail above the water. Tense and snorting, it was obvious the manatee was in pain.

But Amy didn't think she was dying. Billy didn't think so, either.

The manatee sealed her nostrils closed and disappeared in the murk. Perhaps she had sunk to the river bottom to rest. Manatees can stay under water for up to 12 minutes, but they usually come up for air every five. The more active they are, the more often they need to surface.

This was one active manatee. Every few minutes she broke the waterline to breath and arch her back before disappearing again. For the next hour and a half, Gerry and Amy took turns with the video camera. All eyes stayed on the river. It seemed as if every time the cow surfaced she stayed there longer, slapping her tail hard on the water as she bent her back and flared her nostrils.

Amy noticed that the manatee had a large piece, a half-moon shape, missing from her tail. She'd probably had a bad accident with the sharp edges of a motor-boat propeller. The cut was old and had long healed over, but it marked her for life.

At 11:30 a.m. the manatee was at the surface again. This time, though, the cow did not disappear after breathing. Instead, she arched her back, stiffened with strain and held her nose and tail above the water. Five minutes passed ... six ... seven ... At last, with a churning twist, the manatee stirred up the water around her and relaxed.

A small, pale grey balloonish shape appeared beside the enormous cow. Could it be a calf? Amy thought so, but she needed to see a pair of nostrils to be sure. The calf did not cooperate. The new mother disappeared again under the water. Everyone waited. But this time they did not see the manatee come up.

"We've got to get back to the office to call Dean," said Amy. Dean Friedman is one of the pilots who takes the researchers flying over the St. John's River twice a month. During the flights they map the river's manatee population by marking a dot on a map of Jacksonville wherever they see a manatee. It's important work. Knowing where the manatees are at certain times of the year helps the State of Florida manage boat traffic on the river. State officers can advise boaters to slow down or avoid certain parts of the river where manatees gather.

Two hours later Amy was sitting beside Dean in the cockpit of a four-seater Cessna 172. Gerry was in the back seat, adjusting the telephoto lens on his camera. The plane was 152 metres (500 feet) in the air above the St. John's River, heading for the Trout River tributary. The St. John's is a huge, slow-moving river, 580 kilometres (360 miles) long and more than six kilometres (four miles) wide in some places. It's also a dark river — a high concentration of tannic acid from fallen leaves gives the water a brown, tea colour. Pine, oak and cypress trees and marsh grass line its banks. The manatees feed upon the thick carpet of tape grass growing on the river bottom.

There are waterways in Florida as clear as aquamarines. From the sky, manatees are almost easy to count in gem-blue water. And then there's the turbid St. John's and its muddy tributaries, where you can hardly ever get a sure view of anything. At the mouth of the Trout River, dolphins, ducks and herons were half-hidden by the murky water — only the bright white egrets stood out against the bold background.

"There she is!" Amy crowed. Looking through her binoculars, she had found the manatee with the half-moon slice in her tail. She was about 1.5 kilometres (one mile) upriver from where they'd seen her give birth. Swimming close to her side was a white-coloured speck. At birth, manatee calves weigh about 30 kilograms (66 pounds) and measure somewhere between 1.2 and 1.4 metres (four and four-and-a-half feet) long. From the air the calf appeared very small, a star in the shadow of a moon, next to its mammoth mother.

If only they could get a better look. Dean took the plane down to about 120 metres (400 feet). It was as low as they could go. If the plane flew any nearer to the river the noise from its propeller would disturb the cow and calf. Manatee mothers may react to danger by trying to escape and fleeing manatees travel at their top speed: about 24 kilometres (15 miles) an hour. Though the plane could keep up with the manatee, it would only frighten and stress her more.

Dean kept the Cessna steeply banked and flew around and around in tight circles while Gerry snapped pictures of the scene below. On the map in her lap Amy made two black dots, one smaller than the other. She wrote "Half-Moon" beside the larger dot, as a kind of reminder. As if she'd ever forget.

In the months to come, the research team all would spot Half-Moon on separate manatee mapping flights. She was almost always seen with a calf, though they could never be totally, scientifically positive that it belonged to her.

"What a day," Amy thought as the plane touched down on the airstrip. "Quinton's never going to believe this."

But he did. Every word.

She was almost always seen with a calf, though they could never be totally, scientifically positive that it belonged to her.

A pair of manatees surfaces together, muzzle to muzzle.

II

THE SCIENTIST:

A. Quinton White Jr.

D r. Quinton White is a marine biologist with a strong interest in the impact of people on the environment. He has studied many pollution problems and he has learned that crabs, shrimp and manatees are all very good indicators of the health of the environment. He is dean of the College of Arts and Sciences and professor of biology and marine science at Jacksonville University in Jacksonville, Florida. He is also the director of a team of researchers who study manatees in the St. John's River and its tributaries.

Growing up "on the water" in coastal north Virginia, Quinton was always interested in marine biology. "I was always around the water. I spent my childhood around the river, bay and ocean and I spend part of every summer on the Outer Banks of North Carolina.

"I went to college thinking I would be a physician, but absolutely fell in love with teaching. I was very lucky that one of my professors saw something in me and asked me to help teach some labs. It was great!!! I then knew what I wanted to do and decided to go to graduate school to become a professor."

But before he could pursue his dream, a detour of duty sent Quinton to the army and to Vietnam. He returned to complete his Ph.D. at the University of South Carolina at the Baruch Institute for Marine Biology and Coastal Research.

Quinton can still remember his first manatee sighting. It was in 1976, and he was a newly minted professor with classes to teach. "When you're a young professor, all

Quinton White (standing), Amy Robison, and Gerry Pinto at Duval County Manatee Headquarters.

you seem to do is write and give lectures," he says. "One night I went out for a walk. It was a beautiful fall evening, so I headed down to the Jacksonville University dock — right on the St. John's River — to think about a lecture I was preparing." Standing on the dock, Quinton's mind was a million miles away when a loud "raspberry noise" broke into his quiet thoughts. "I looked down, heard a *big* exhale, and then a manatee surfaced. Its head bobbed out of the water and it scared the bejeebies out of me!" he recalls. "I laughed when I realized what it was."

Quinton's marine science research has led him to China, South America, the Galapagos Islands, the Bahamas and Australia. While most of his research is done on the surface of the sea, he has been down to 450 metres (1,500 feet) in the Johnson-Sea Link submersible to do research on deep-sea crabs. He can sum up his whole career path in nine words: he knows for sure that "I just followed what came very naturally to me."

III

THE SCIENCE:

Manatee Mapping

I n the early 1990s, the State of Florida proposed a conservation plan to help protect all its endangered manatees. At the time, a member of the Jacksonville City Council went to Quinton White's office to ask what he knew about manatees and what he thought of the plan. That was the beginning of Quinton's research on manatees.

His earliest findings showed that not a whole lot was known about manatees in northeast Florida and, unfortunately, the government's protection measures were based on observations of manatees in the south of the state. They wouldn't work in the north of the state, where manatee movement patterns were different.

> The research provided a foundation for a regional manatee protection plan to reduce human-caused disturbance to manatees.

For more than 10 years, manatee mapping by researchers at Jacksonville University has sharpened the picture of manatee movement, population patterns and how humans impact their lives in Florida's northeast. The research provided a foundation for a regional manatee protection plan to reduce human-caused disturbance to manatees. As part of the plan, boaters or jet skiers must keep their craft at least 15 metres (50 feet) from a manatee; they need to wear polarized sunglasses while on the water to increase their chances of spotting manatees before they get too close; and they must respect signage along the waterways, particularly the no entry zone sign, which prohibits boating, jet skiing and swimming in sensitive manatee habitats.

Research also confirmed that it isn't just motorboats and jet skis that can bring danger to manatees. People who feed manatees may cause them to lose their innate fear of humans; loud noises and splashing are frightening to a manatee's sensitive hearing; and manatees may defend themselves if they feel harassed or chased when they are leaving an area. So, just like boaters, swimmers need to keep it down and maintain their distance.

> People who feed manatees may cause them to lose their innate fear of humans; loud noises and splashing are frightening to a manatee's sensitive hearing; and manatees may defend themselves if they feel harassed or chased when they are leaving an area.

The mapping has proved Quinton's theory that manatee mothers move into tributaries to give birth. As a result, protection in those areas has been increased.

It isn't just outdoor-lovers who have to abide by the rules and keep their distance. "We do virtually no in-water work with manatees," says Quinton of his researchers. "We want to have as little impact on the manatees as possible." Instead, the research team rely on their in-flight observations and on calls to the manatee hotline to report sightings.

Apart from giving manatees their space, the hands-off approach of manatee mapping has been a boon for understanding the migrations of other species. "We've seen a lot of porpoises, sharks, rays and even loggerhead sea turtles from the plane," says Quinton. "And we saw that eagle rays congregate off the coast of Jacksonville for mating — we didn't know they occurred there before."

IV

THE ANIMAL NOTES:

Florida

Manatee

Common name:	Florida manatee	Family:	Trichechidae
Scientific name:	*Trichechus manatus latirostris*	Genus:	*Trichechus*
		Species:	*manatus*
Order:	Sirenia	Sub Species:	*latirostris*
Suborder:	Sirenia		

Scientists believe that *Trichechus manatus latirostris* is a subspecies of the West Indian Manatee, *Trichechus Manatus.*

Size/weight:

At birth manatees weigh about 30 kilograms (66 pounds) and measure between 1.2 and 1.4 metres (four to four-and-a-half feet). They can grow up to 3.66 metres (12 feet) long, weighing up to 900 kilograms (2,000 pounds). Females are bigger than males.

Description:

The manatee has a large, grey-brown, seal-like body with two front flippers and wrinkled head, big, **prehensile** lips and large nostrils surrounded by whiskers

Reproduction:

Manatees form mating groups, with one female, or cow, followed by a dozen or more males, or bulls. Manatees usually bear one calf every three to five years, travelling into quiet waterways to give birth.

Food:

A full-grown manatee can eat between 45 and 90 kilograms (100 and 200 pounds) of water plants a day. Constant grubbing in the sand for food wears down their teeth; new ones grow in at the back of their mouths and gradually work their way forward.

Approximate lifespan:

Manatees live about 60 years.

Status:

Florida's manatees are protected from hunting, but much of their sea grass habitat has been destroyed by pollution and riverside development. The West Indian manatee was once abundant throughout the North and South American Atlantic and Caribbean waters but its numbers have been greatly reduced through much of this range. Because adult manatees grow to be so large, they become too big for natural predators to take them on. They are at risk for accidents with motorboat propellers and fishing gear. Biologists estimate there are 2,600 to 2,800 manatees in Florida, and approximately one-third of them can be identified by scars or skin discolorations.

Habitat:

Manatees live in shallow, slow-moving rivers, bays and coastal waters where sunlight promotes plant growth, in either fresh or salt water. They require sheltered living and breeding areas, a steady food supply and warm water.

Range/Distribution:

Florida manatees specifically are found on the coast of Florida; West Indian manatees range from Florida south into the Amazon region.

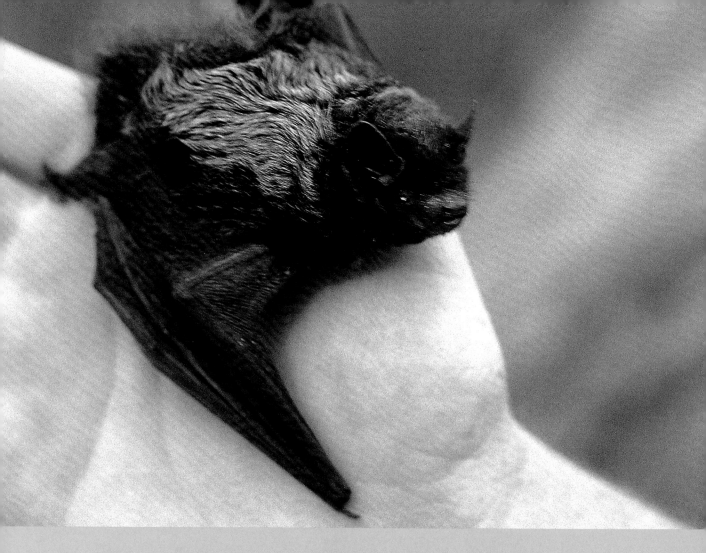

Bats are easily injured by people. It takes special training to learn how to handle and not hurt them, or get hurt.

The silver-haired bat is so called because of the patch of dense, white-tipped hair on its back.

Bat-tized

I

O n a clear, dry evening in May 1997, bat biologist Janet Tyburec was getting ready to teach bat-handling and bat identification. Her classroom was the Chiricahua Mountains in southeastern Arizona. Her students were three biologists, experts in the wild animals and plants in the desert mountain range, but none of them had any experience working with bats.

LESSON NUMBER 1: Reproductive female bats need the most fuel and therefore the most prey-rich habitats. By comparison, non-reproductive females and males eat less each night, so they can get by in habitat where prey is not as abundant or diverse.

LESSON NUMBER 2: To conserve their energy, pregnant and **lactating** female bats often form maternity roosts, or bat nurseries, near prey-rich habitat. If biologists catch females early in the night, they can get an idea of where to find prey-rich habitat and maternity roosts.

LESSON NUMBER 3: To protect habitat for threatened or endangered bats, understanding the needs of the reproducing females is top priority. Their lifestyles cover the critical habitat essential to supporting the species.

Bats need safe **foraging** areas, day roosts and night roosts, and bat mothers need isolated places to rear their young. To protect a bat habitat, biologists need to know not only where their insect prey gathers, but also where the nurseries are. And finding bugs is not half as hard as finding bat babies. In fact, bats are so good at squeezing themselves into holes in trees and rocks, and into cracks and crevices that scientists don't know where the bat nurseries of more than half the world's bats are hidden. The problem is, it's hard to protect a bat nursery from people if you don't know where it is in the first place.

> Scientists don't know where the bat nurseries of more than half the world's bats are hidden.

One of the best places to find bats in the Chiricahuas is over the slow-moving parts of the stream that runs through Cave Creek Canyon. Where the stream flows slowly and silently, bats can hunt above it without getting their signals jammed by the sounds of rushing water.

Janet chose a spot where a dense stand of sycamore trees grew on either side of the stream and created a clear, tunnel-like route under the forest canopy for bats to easily fly through. The four biologists unrolled a pair of mist nets across the stream and secured the ends to tall poles, tethered to the ground. They looked like two gigantic volleyball nets, except that the black nylon netting was much finer.

Once the mist nets were set up, there was nothing for the group to do but sit

Even the sound of a boot scraping on the rocky ground could alert bats to a human presence and send them flying off in another direction.

Janet and her students take a closer look at the bat they've caught and easily identify it as a silver-haired.

down beside the poles and wait. They all switched off their headlamps and tried not to make any noise.

Janet concentrated on sitting perfectly still and keeping one finger on a main strand of the net. Even the sound of a boot scraping on the rocky ground could alert bats to a human presence and send them flying off in another direction.

To find their way around in the dark, bats use echolocation. They emit high-frequency sounds from their mouths or nostrils to detect obstacles like rocks, branches, shrubbery and prey in their paths. When the sound waves hit something, they bounce back to the bat like an echo, giving them an idea of what's ahead. A bat's **echolocation** is so well tuned that it can detect even the super-fine strands of a mist net. Fortunately for bat biologists, bats have a tendency to get used to the same flyways and not bother to echolocate in them for new barriers.

"Sproiiiiiiiiiiiiiinnnnnng!" the strand of net jerked under Janet's finger. She leaped to her feet and popped on her headlamp .

"Ker ... plop!"

Oops. The net had been set a little too tight. A bat bounced off it and fell with a splash into the stream.

Fortunately, bats are excellent swimmers. Although most kinds of bats aren't strong enough to take off into flight from the water, they do the butterfly stroke like champions.

The biologists traced the direction the bat was swimming in and hurried to meet it at the water's edge. They couldn't waste a second — a bat on the ground waiting to dry before takeoff is an easy meal for a raccoon or another night hunter. As the bat pulled itself out of the stream and shook some of the water out of its soggy fur, Janet slid a glove onto her left hand, reached down and picked it up. The bat was a female, and by her appearance, in her pup-bearing years. She folded her wings against her body, nibbled a bit on Janet's glove and shivered. Before they could do any kind of identification Janet had to get the bat warm and dry, so she stretched out the neck of her sweatshirt and tucked the bat inside, where she clutched the front of Janet's undershirt with her feet and settled into the soft fleece.

"She recognizes I'm giving her a place to warm up, that's why she's so calm," Janet explained to the other biologists. The group left the stream bed and followed the light from their headlamps up to where Janet's truck was parked. As Janet was laying out the transmitter equipment on the tailgate of the truck, she felt the bat stir and right herself, then claw her way across the undershirt, heading toward Janet's left shoulder. Janet felt a warm little trickle down her sleeve as the tiny bat urinated on her arm.

As soon as the bat was finished, she clawed her way back to the front of Janet's T-shirt, swivelled upside down again and went back to sleep.

It wasn't the first time Janet had been "bat-tized." Sometimes they urinated on her, sometimes they made a couple of grain-sized droppings. Really, it was no big deal, she explained to her grimacing crew. Bats have very clean habits and they groom themselves every day, much like a cat does. To void, they will either "let go" in flight or, if they're hanging out, they'll move to a different part of the roost to do their business.

> **It wasn't the first time Janet had been "bat-tized."**

They don't like to soil themselves either, so if they're hanging upside down by their feet, they always right themselves before going, by turning around and hanging from the thumb claws of their wings. That way the urine or **guano** falls free and doesn't dirty their fur.

About a half hour after getting dunked in the stream, the bat was warm and dry. Janet removed her from her sweatshirt and inspected her. She showed the others how to use an identification key to match the bat with her species. Janet already knew the kinds of bats that could be found in the canyon, narrowing their choices down from more than 1,000 species worldwide to 20 local species.

The bat had fuzzy, black fur, tipped with silver, and small ears. It also had a wide, dark, hairless muzzle — like a little buffalo. A very little buffalo. The bat weighed only 10 grams (about the same as two nickels or a small handfull of M & Ms). Janet worked through her checklist and concluded that she had a silver-haired bat in her hand. She was relieved it wasn't a hoary bat. Hoary's are harder to handle than their smaller, silver-haired cousins, and they have a snapping-good bite.

Janet clipped a reflector band to the bat's forearm, on the leading edge of its wing. She was pleased they'd caught a young female: she'd be a good bat to tag with a radio transmitter and she just might lead them to the nursery.

Janet activated the battery for a tiny, 0.6-gram transmitter that would be glued to the bat's back. To keep the bat from pulling it off before the glue dried, she rolled the little animal up, burrito-style, in a clean bandana and held it in her hand. Wrapped up with only her face showing, the bat looked at Janet, blinked a few times and fell asleep.

While the bat slept, the team scouted the area for a good place to set her free. They couldn't just toss her into the air — that would really freak her out. Back at the stream they found a low tree branch for the bat to perch on while it pulled itself together.

When the glue was dry, Janet unrolled the bat burrito and placed the silver-haired gently on the branch. For a moment the bat just sat there. Then she raised her head and opened her mouth, but nobody could hear the sound she made. "She's echolocating," Janet whispered to the others, "just getting her bearings back."

Ignoring the four headlamps pointing at her, the bat unfurled her wings and began to groom herself, trying to dislodge the transmitter. When she realized it wasn't coming off she jumped into the air. The biologists watched her fly away until her reflector wing-band disappeared into the dark. It was close to midnight. The bat still had a few good hours to forage.

For the next few days, Janet and her students kept busy tracking the silver-haired. Radio transmitters for bats last no longer than two weeks. Eventually the "batpack" falls off after the animal's next molting and the bat shows no signs of ever having been tagged. Sometimes Janet got a bearing on her up in the mountains, where the cliffs were too steep to climb. At other times the bat made a day roost in a tree in the forest. Then there were times Janet didn't know where she was

"I never thought I would be working with animals, never saw myself as an animal handler," she says. "Mainly because I hate the thought of getting bitten." And some bats do bite.

Janet clips the fur from the silver-haired bat before attaching the transmitter.

at all. Each day, the team tried to get a bearing on the bat as she headed off to her roost at dawn. After breakfast and a short nap, the team would head off to try to locate and describe the bat's day roost.

Three nights later, Janet was lying in her sleeping bag on a narrow ridge halfway up one of the mountains in the Chiricahua range. It was too windy to pitch a tent, so she'd tied her backpack, hiking boots and radio-tracking equipment to a nearby manzanita bush to keep them from blowing away. She had her radio receiver on, her headlamp was strapped to her head and, in case she fell asleep, the alarm clock by her head was set for 4 a.m. — about the time that bats would be returning to their day roosts.

A new moon that night lit up the sky and a meteorite show was playing over the mountains. There were so many stars that even someone who'd slept under a thousand night skies would have been amazed. Janet wanted to stay awake, but she hadn't slept much since they'd tagged the silver-haired. Even the wind whipping and whining through the scrubby bushes couldn't keep her eyes open ...

"Boop ..." sounded softly from the speaker.

"Boop ..." There it was again.

"Boop ... boop ... boop ..." The signals were getting louder and stronger.

Janet was wide awake now. She popped on her headlamp, sat up straight, arched her neck and scanned the night sky.

"BOOP! ... BOOP! ... BOOP! ... BOOP! ... BOOP!"

When the silver-haired passed over Janet's head, the sounds coming from the loudspeaker peaked, sharp and clear. Janet caught the reflector band in the beam of her headlamp and followed the bat with her gaze. As the bat flew out of reach of the light beam and beyond, into the dark sky, it looked to Janet as if she was watching a meteorite streaking across the canyon.

Janet noted the direction in which the bat was travelling, but wasn't sure where she was heading. An abandoned woodpecker hole? A cavity inside a dead tree? A tiny rock crevice? Wherever her day roost was, and wherever she might one day have her pup, remained a secret between the bat and the stars.

II

THE SCIENTIST:
Janet Tyburec

"I never really thought much about bats as a child," says Janet Tyburec. "I don't remember learning about them in school until I was in junior high, and we didn't have books like *Stellaluna* and *Silverwing* to inspire us."

Janet grew up in Milwaukee, Wisconsin, and she's pretty sure she spent more time out of doors than in. Some of her earliest memories are of walks in the woods, puddle-bugging in creeks and ponds and burrowing deep in snowbanks to make cities in winter.

When she was 12, her family moved to Tucson, Arizona, where the sun shines 300 or more days a year — great weather for an outdoor explorer like Janet. In junior high school in Tucson she had a science teacher who introduced his students to the flora and fauna of the desert where they lived, and that included bats. Janet remembers that her teacher never presented bats as scary creatures that come out on Halloween, but as animals who shared their desert home.

Thinking she wanted to be a veterinarian, Janet chose to spend a high-school career day at a vet's practice. That one day in a closed building with dog and cat dander thick in the air left her wheezing and re-evaluating her options. "That was when I decided to study plants. They weren't full of asthma-inducing **dander**, they didn't bite and you didn't have to chase them down before working on them.

"In college, I took all the natural history, botany, plant physiology and ecology classes I could. Upon graduation I got a summer job as a field assistant on a National Geographic-funded research project to study the reproductive biology of columnar cacti in Mexico. The cacti we were studying were pollinated by bats. And it was in the desert along the Sea of Cortez that I handled my first bat. I was hooked."

Janet has a degree in biology and English from Trinity University in San Antonio, Texas. She has been studying bats for more than 15 years and has handled more than 13,000 of them. Her work has taken her to the deserts and forests of Mexico, the tropical forests of Belize, Costa Rica and Peru and the savannahs of East Africa. All told, she's had first-hand encounters with about 250 different species of bats.

"I never thought I would be working with animals, never saw myself as an animal handler," she says. "Mainly because I hate the thought of getting bitten." And some bats do bite. "You have to know what you're doing in handling a bat. And it helps to remember that you're bigger than they are." But when she thinks of a species like the pallid bat (*Antrozous pallidus*), known to wrestle down a scorpion before eating it, it's hard even for Janet not to feel a little intimidated. Still, pallids are probably her favourite bat. "Pallid bats are like the Arnold Schwarzeneggers of the bat world. They are big and tough. They are not cute or pretty like winsome flying foxes, but they are charismatic."

As the education programs director for Bat Conservation International (www.batcon.org) in Austin, Texas, Janet often found herself in classrooms clearing up myths and misconceptions about bats. "They aren't blind, they don't get tangled in your hair, they don't all carry rabies and they aren't rodents," are some of the biggies. Forget what you thought about bats and full moons — most bats are "lunarphobic," tending to avoid flying along open areas when the moon is bright. There is good reason for their phobia: Under a full moon, bats are much more obvious to owls and other nocturnal predators.

Janet says that, apart from not being afraid of the dark, "bat researchers must be patient, quiet, observant and have a high tolerance for boredom. Studying bats is often much like fishing — you are never guaranteed to capture or even see the target species."

Janet says that, apart from not being afraid of the dark, "bat researchers must be patient, quiet, observant and have a high tolerance for boredom."

Janet Tyburec carefully removes the bat from the mist net.

III

THE SCIENCE:

Echolocation: Seeing in the Dark

It was way back in the late 1700s that an Italian scientist named Lazzaro Spallanzani began to figure out why bats were so good at getting around in the dark. Spallanzani tried an experiment: he put an owl and a bat in a pitch-black room to see what would happen. While the bat flew about effortlessly, the owl bumped into things. But when Spallanzani covered the bat's head, it lost its power to navigate in the dark.

Spallanzani and his colleagues progressed as far as figuring out that a bat could "see" using sound. For 150 years, not much progress was made on Spallanzani's untested hypothesis that bats used hearing to "see in the dark." It wasn't until the 1930s that a student at Harvard University named Donald R. Griffith used specially designed microphones to show that bats produce calls outside the range of human hearing, and the echoes from those calls bounce back to give them an impression of objects in their flight path.

Now, in the 21st century, research continues into the intricacies of echolocation. Scientists have discovered that many factors come into play for bats to hear a "picture" of their surrounding objects and prey. For one thing, some bats use their vocal cords to produce echolocation calls, while others use the click of their tongues. Different species of bats emit different frequencies of sounds — some low enough to fall into the range of human hearing (we can pick up frequencies in the range of 20 kilohertz or lower). They do this so that their echolocation falls outside the range of what their insect prey can hear. Still, some insects are able to foil bats by jamming bat calls with high-pitched calls of their own. And there are bats, such as pallid bats, that aren't known to use echolocation to locate prey. "Pallids listen to the rustling sounds made by the footsteps or other movement of their prey. Their ears are tuned to listen to sounds between five and 100 kilohertz, with maximum sensitivity in the lower frequency ranges." The three- to eight-kilohertz sounds made by a crawling insect are right at peak sensitivity for a pallid bat to hear. Not all sounds made by bats are technically considered "**echolocation**" calls. Bats make a number of vocalization sounds, including **echolocation**, but some calls are used to communicate with other bats. Some of these "social calls" are below 15-20 kilohertz (kHz) in frequency and may be audible to humans. Most bat echolocation calls are also very loud, says Janet. They are so intense that if we could hear them, they would sound like a smoke alarm.

Bats that hunt flying prey tend to produce longer, broadband calls (calls that sweep through a series of frequencies) to give them "the big picture" of what's in their flight path. As they get closer to their prey, their calls get narrower (sweeping through fewer frequencies) and are sent closer together, to help them zero in on the details of their prey. Bats that hunt wingless prey also use echolocation, but more to get their bearings.

How is it then that bats with such sophisticated **echolocation** abilities ever get bungled up in mist nets? "We try to intercept bats along regular flyways where they are used to travelling," explains Janet. "The theory is that bats will get lazy about using their echolocation in an area they have used frequently because they are not expecting to run into a finely threaded net. Instead, they are simply keying in on big objects such as trees and the ground. It's like when people travel along regular routes, say to and from work — they get complacent about their commute and don't notice a new traffic sign until a police officer pulls them over. Bat biologists with their camouflaged mist nets are like cops hiding behind billboards with radar guns." Most of the bats Janet has caught in her career have been quick learners — catch them once, maybe. Catch them twice? Not very likely.

IV

Silver-

haired Bat

Common name:	silver-haired bat	Family:	Vespertilionidae
Scientific name:	*Lasionycteris noctivagans*	Genus:	*Lasionycteris*
		Species:	*noctivagans*
Order:	Chiroptera		

Bats have been on the planet for 50 million-plus years. With more than 1,000 different kinds in existence today, there's a bat species adapted to almost any habitat on earth, except in the most extreme desert and polar environments.

Size/weight:

The silver-haired bat averages about 10 grams (0.3 ounces) in weight, has a total body length of 100 millimetres (4 inches) and a wingspread of 270 to 310 millimetres (11 inches).

Description:

The silver-haired bat has rich chocolate brown fur with silver-frosted hairs on the back, belly and tail membranes. It has small ears and a wide, dark, hairless muzzle. Clocked at nearly 18 kilometres (11 miles) an hour, it is one of the slowest-flying bats of its region, making it easier to identify on the wing.

Reproduction:

In spring the female awakens from hibernation, pregnant from fall breeding, to migrate farther north for the summer. Females bare their two young in late spring or early summer, when the insect population is high. Bat nurseries are squeezed into holes in rocks and trees and into cracks and crevices.

Food:

Insects are captured in flight by the teeth or wing tip and eaten while the bat is flying. If a bat is doing well it can catch hundreds of moths, beetles and other bugs each night. Bats fly over quiet waterways, finding insects by echolocation (emitting high-frequency sounds from their mouths or nostrils).

Approximate lifespan:

The silver-haired bat has a lifespan of at least 12 years.

Status:

The silver-haired bat is one of the most abundant bats in forested areas of the northern United States and Canada. However, clearcutting, accompanied by the disposal of dead trees, threatens the habitat the silver-haired needs for survival.

Habitat:

Silver-haired bats roost in trees near lakes and streams in wooded areas. Generally roosts are under the loose bark of trees, in hollow trees or burrowed into large birds' nests, but they can also be found in rock crevices.

Range/distribution:

Bats have been on the planet for 50 million-plus years. With more than 1,000 different kinds in existence today, there's a bat species adapted to almost any habitat on earth, except in the most extreme desert and polar environments. The silver-haired bat is unique to North America; it is found in southwestern Alaska, southern Canada and throughout the United States. Males and females have different ranges in the summer; the females migrate north for the summer, while males and females winter together in the south.

So many gannets nested there that from a distance it appeared as if the cliffs were covered in snow.

Living, breathing gannets nesting among the cliff tops on the Île aux Perroquets.

A Flurry of Gannets

June 8, 1997

On a Maine highway, a cargo van driven by Kathleen Blanchard was heading north for Île aux Perroquets in the Mingan archipelago along the Quebec North Shore. Kathleen knew how to get there because she'd been to the island before. She knew the island's story well and all about how its once-magnificent colony of northern gannets had entirely disappeared.

"Island of the Parrots" was named for the puffins, sometimes called "sea parrots," that nest every summer in burrows on the island's cliffs. Two hundred years ago it might just as well have been

> **With the help of other concerned seabird conservationists, Kathleen got the Canadian government's permission to do the study.**

called "Island of the Gannets."

In the 19th century, naturalists visiting Île aux Perroquets recorded seeing an immense colony of gannets on the high cliffs. So many gannets nested there that from a distance it appeared as if the cliffs were covered in snow. But overhunting, egg-collecting and human disturbance took a terrible toll on the gannet population in the western North Atlantic. The last recorded sighting of a small number of gannets on Île aux Perroquets was in 1887, the same year the first light station was built on the island.

Around this time, gannets were also **extirpated** from the gannetry near Grand Manan, New Brunswick in 1886 and the colony rear Yarmouth, Nova Scotia in 1880.

In 1918 the Migratory Bird Treaty Act between Canada and the United States gave gannets official protection, but in all the years since then they have not made a comeback on Île aux Perroquets. If gannets were going to return to the island, humans would have to help them.

After many years of planning and preparation, Kathleen was on her way to try to tempt them back.

As president of the Quebec-Labrador Foundation in Canada, Kathleen worked with Richard Sears of the Mingan Island Cetacean Study to set up the northern gannet restoration project for Île aux Perroquets. With the help of other concerned seabird conservationists, Kathleen got the Canadian government's permission to do the study and organized fundraising for the project.

In Maine, Kathleen stopped to pick up one of her biggest supporters, ornithologist Steve Kress, director of the seabird restoration program for the National Audubon Society. Steve had with him gannet decoys, dozens of them. Because there were no real gannets on Île aux Perroquets, decoys were needed to stand in their place.

Together, Kathleen and Steve loaded 46 individually wrapped decoys into the

After many years of planning and preparation, Kathleen was on her way to try to tempt them back.

Minga sets the decoys up on the cliffs hoping they'll attract some real gannets back to the island.

van. They had worked together before. Twenty-four years earlier, with the support of the Canadian Wildlife Service, Steve and a team of research assistants began relocating Atlantic puffin chicks from a colony on Great Island, Newfoundland, to Eastern Egg Rock off the coast of Maine. As with the gannets of Île aux Perroquets, overhunting **extirpated** the original puffin colony on Egg Rock. All but two of the puffin colonies on nearby islands had also disappeared, for the same reason.

Every summer for the next several years, "Project Puffin" continued to relocate Great Island chicks to Eastern Egg Rock and to nearby Seal Island. Today there are established puffin nesting colonies on both Eastern Egg Rock and Seal Island; their numbers are small but growing steadily.

Back in the 1970s, Kathleen was the first field assistant Steve hired for Project Puffin. Now she had a project of her own and she needed Steve's help to set it up properly.

There's no better magnet to a puffin than another puffin. The same is true for gannets. That's why the decoys were so important, and they had to be good ones. They had to look just like gannets.

Each of Steve's life-size decoys had been hand-painted to match the colours of an adult gannet: pure white body with black primary feathers on each wing, pale yellow head, grey-blue feet and beak, and ice blue eyes. Some decoys were modelled standing up, others were fashioned in an incubating pose. Steve also had a CD player (complete with solar cell batteries to generate power from the sun) to play recordings of gannet cries.

The cargo van crossed the border and continued north. At Matapedia in Quebec Kathleen picked up her last passenger, a young ecologist and environmental researcher named Minga O'Brien. Minga had worked on various field research projects and was now going to live on the island to watch and record the comings and goings of gannets that summer.

When they arrived at Longue-Pointe-de-Mingan the following day, Richard Sears was waiting for them. The next day, he was going to take Kathleen, Steve, Minga and all their cargo across to the island in the inflatable Zeppelin boat that he used to study whales in the Gulf of St. Lawrence. The boat belonged to the Mingan Island Cetacean Study (MICS for short). Richard is the director of MICS and he promised that someone from the group would take Minga back to the mainland whenever she asked them to, and they would check in on her sometimes to see how she was doing.

June 11, 1997, Île aux Perroquets, Mingan Archipelago Reserve National Park, Gulf of St. Lawrence, Quebec, Canada

Puffins waddled on the rocks and fluttered about in the wind. A pair of ravens darted through the air, eiders paddled in the nearshore waters and terns waded along the shoreline.

Kathleen, Steve, Richard and Minga unwrapped the decoys and arranged them along the edge of the cliff, about six metres above the sea. With beaks pointed west, into the prevailing winds, the decoys faced the sea and waited. In this position they would appear to make eye contact with any real gannets carried on the wind currents from the huge Bonaventure colony about 160 kilometres (100 miles) away, as the gannet flies.

August 4, 1997

Minga was alone on Île aux Perroquets. Sort of. She shared her summer camp with nesting Atlantic puffins, razorbills, spotted sandpipers, tree swallows and savannah sparrows. At low tide a ring of flat rock ledges around the island invited whimbrels, short-billed dowitchers, greater and lesser yellowlegs, red knots, plovers and ruddy turnstones down to scuttle upon the shelf. In good weather, when the sea was calm, boats brought tourists from the mainland. Volunteers took turns keeping Minga company and her mom was with her now. Every five or seven days Minga caught a ride back to the mainland for groceries, fresh water, some conversation and a shower.

Seven-and-a-half weeks had passed since Minga first arrived on the island. Sometimes she would see hundreds of gannets in the air — though they never landed. It didn't take long before many of the decoys were covered in streaks and splotches of white gannet guano.

At 11:37 a.m., sitting with her mother on the pavement of the island's helicopter launch pad, Minga wrote history in her journal:

"Adult gannet landed in the southwest corner of the decoys; right at the edge of the cliff. Has been preening himself ..." Twenty minutes later, the gannet moved into the flock of decoys and "appeared to be sleeping."

The gannet preened, snoozed and yawned the next hour away. Once, he scratched his head with his foot. At 12:54 the gannet "popped up his head, faced edge of cliff and flew west."

Minga was thrilled. She decided to call her first visitor "Fergus le Fou," a play on the French nickname for gannet, "Fou de Bassan," which means "the crazy of Bass Rock." Bass Rock lies off the coast of Scotland and is home to one of the world's most famous gannetries.

August 5, 1997

"Overcast with a few clear periods, very little wind," Minga wrote in her log. For Minga, a break from the wind was a relief. A gannet's body fat helps protect it from the cold but Minga didn't have a gannet's insulation. Every day, she sat at her observation post at the top of the lighthouse, just under the light, wearing mittens, a couple of sweaters and long johns under her jeans. The automated lighthouse was good only for gannet-watching and food storage — it was too cold and damp inside for a shelter.

In early July Minga was given permission to sleep in the emergency cabin. Before that she had camped in a tent outside; when it was time for bed, she crawled into her doubled-up sleeping bag and prayed that the wind wouldn't pull the tent off its pegs and drag her off the island while she slept.

August 15, 1997

Summers are cold and windy enough in the North Atlantic, but winters can be brutal. Gannets are hardy birds but even they need to escape the north in winter. On this morning, Minga had to leave Île aux Perroquets for the last time. She had other work to begin back home in Halifax.

In the future, if gannets chose to nest on Île aux Perroquets the young birds reared there would probably return to the island as five-year-olds to begin their own breeding cycle. Gannets had already shown a strong interest in the island, but Minga knew that for the project to succeed the local people must support it for a long time to come. Visitors to the island would have to keep disturbance to a minimum. As she stepped into the boat for the last time she let out a worried sigh — she had to leave, yet the struggle to restore the gannetry while respecting the people whose lives involved the island was just beginning.

As the Zeppelin took off from shore, a flock gathered over Minga's head. In all her trips back and forth from the mainland, Fergus and the other "fous" hadn't shown much interest in the boat. Now Minga looked up at the flurry of gannets and felt her spirits lift a little with the many wingbeats and the change in the weather.

September 3, 1997, Quebec-Labrador Foundation office, Montreal, Quebec
Kathleen lifted her eyes from her reading. From the window of her office overlooking the St. Lawrence River she could see gulls and cormorants circling in the air. On her desk lay Minga's journal — the notes on the **guano**-bombed decoys, Fergus and the other gannets that followed him ... the gannets passing, circling, landing ... the fog, the wind, the wet ...

Between the lines of Minga's entries Kathleen realized there was something familiar about the report. It was a link in a long chain that had begun many years ago, when Kathleen herself was a young intern on Project Puffin. Information from that restoration, gathered over so many years, had been passed on to help the gannet project. Next summer, there would be a new intern, and the knowledge from this first field study to pass on. With every passing year the pile of journals would grow. If, one day, gannets took hold and nested on Île aux Perroquets, then the record of what was possible first for puffins, then for gannets, would be ready to help bring another seabird colony back from the brink.

II

The Scientist:
Kathleen
Blanchard

"I was always interested in nature," says Kathleen Blanchard. "Even when I was very young, I lived for it. My Dad was from Newfoundland and that gave him a very strong connection with the land and the sea. It was something he passed on to me.

"Professionally, my first big break was in working for the National Audubon Society. I was 19 when I got a summer job working at their Adult Ecology Camp. I was glad to be there. I understood, even that young, that I could learn from nature and I wanted to be in the company of great naturalists who could teach me."

While she was at the camp Kathleen had a chance to prove herself. She didn't have any degrees, nor was she zealously trying to save the world. "It was the early '70s, and I was steeped in the philosophy of natural wonder that the writer Rachel Carson inspired in so many people. I was just so keen to learn, and at the same time I wanted to teach others."

It was just the spirit ornithologist Steve Kress was looking for — he hired Kathleen to be the first field assistant on Project Puffin.

Three degrees later, much of Kathleen's work today involves helping government agencies, businesses and conservationists to use environmental education and community-based approaches to tackle conservation programs.

"There's a lot that doesn't come up in college," says Kathleen, who received her Ph.D. from Cornell University in 1984 and has 25 years of seabird conservation work on the Quebec North Shore. "If you work in the field of conservation biology, you need to learn on the job how important it is to garner community support, and how

Kathleen Blanchard and Minga O'Brian sit among the decoys looking for signs of returning birds.

"I was always interested in nature; even when I was very young, I lived for it."

to communicate face to face with local people. We go through school and we think we need to learn all about the animals we are studying, but that is not enough. And at some point you have to be entrepreneurial if you want to make a project happen, even if others don't always agree with you."

III

THE SCIENCE:
Seabird Restoration

Location, location, location. When considering a place to attempt gannet restoration, Kathleen Blanchard and her team needed to find the most promising location they could. Île aux Perroquets was in a region where the gannet population was on the increase and the island itself had a long history as a gannet nesting site, plenty of mackerel in late summer for parent gannets to feed their young, no natural predators and the protection of Parks Canada. What more could a gannet want?

The conditions are good on Île aux Perroquets but nobody was expecting an overnight sensation. After all, the reason Steve Kress happened to have 50 gannet decoys to lend to Kathleen was because he'd tried for several years to bring back gannets along the coast of Maine, without any luck.

"Sometimes we have to work slowly and be patient," says Kathleen. "Social attraction with decoys is the most natural, the most gentle approach we could take, so that is how we began. So if you can succeed without bringing in and rearing chicks from another colony, you try. The drawback is that results can take a very long time and it's hard to teach people to 'wait and see.' Everyone wants results. The donors who fund your study, the interns who observe, the government officials who gave you permits, your colleagues in the scientific community and especially the people in the communities where you work, because you can't bring back the birds without the cooperation and goodwill of the people."

In 1998, the second year of the gannet restoration project, field biologists noted hundreds of gannets flying past Île aux Perroquets on a daily basis. Some days, the fly-bys numbered in the thousands. And there were 15 journals reporting one particularly prospecting gannet pulling grasses — a behaviour that harkens towards nest-building.

Kathleen envisions that the next phase of gannet restoration on Île aux Perroquets will be to translocate chicks from the colony on Bonaventure Island in Quebec's Gaspé Peninsula. "It will more likely lead to a quicker response, which is what we saw with Project Puffin."

The principle behind translocating chicks is "start them while they're young."Translocating is more invasive, but its potential for success is strong because it follows a gannet's natural behaviours and life cycle.They breed every year, usually after the age of five, and are loyal to the same mate year after year. They're also loyal to their nesting site, so where a gannet is raised is where it's most likely to rear its first chick, and the one after, and the one after that Gannets head south for the winter and some fly as far as the Gulf of Mexico. But every year, when they head north in mid-April, they're heading right back to the site where they were born.

Gannets head south for the winter and some fly as far as the Gulf of Mexico.

IV

THE ANIMAL NOTES:

Northern

Gannet

Common name:	northern gannet	Family:	Sulidae
Scientific name:	*Morus bassanus*	Genus:	*Morus*
Order:	*Procellariiformes*	Species:	*bassanus*

Today six gannet breeding colonies remain in the northeast Atlantic, all in Canada. There are approximately 87,900 breeding gannets, not very many as seabird populations go.

Size/weight:

The northern gannet is about the size of a large goose. It grows to 87 to 100 centimetres (35 to 40 inches) in length; the wingspan of an adult bird may be almost two metres (six-and-a-half feet).

Description:

The adult gannet has a dazzling white body with black primary feathers on each wing, a pale yellow head, grey-blue feet and beak and ice blue eyes. Young gannets are brown, becoming whiter as they mature.

Reproduction:

Northern gannets start their breeding cycle at about five years old. Usually the first breeding season is devoted to courtship and building the nest; pairs may remain together for years. A single egg is laid between late May and mid-June and the parent birds take turns incubating the egg with their webbed feet.

Food:

Northern gannets feed on small sea fish such as herring, mackerel, caplin and squid.

Approximate Lifespan:

Gannets live about 16 years.

Status:

Overhunting, egg-collecting and human disturbance took a toll on gannet numbers. Today six gannet breeding colonies remain in the northeast Atlantic, all in Canada. There are approximately 87,900 breeding gannets, not very many as seabird populations go. Another 444, 000 northern gannets nest at 34 colonies on the other side of the Atlantic.

Habitat:

Gannetries are located on steep cliffs and small offshore islands. Ideally, the nesting birds cannot be reached by land predators; if disturbed, gannets will often desert their nests permanently. When wind currents meet a cliff, the current streams upward and carries windsurfing gannets right to the top. A high cliff gives maximum impact to their fishing dives: a gannet diving from 30 metres (100 feet) can make a splash that sends water as far as three metres (10 feet) from where it spears the surface.

Range/distribution:

There are six colonies in the northeast Atlantic, with birds migrating south to disperse along the North American coast from New England to the Gulf of Mexico. In the northwest Atlantic, gannets have colonies in Iceland, the British Isles, including Ireland and the Shetland Islands, and in the Faeroe Islands.

"You want to do everything you can to avoid getting slapped," Molly says. "A flipper slap hurts like you wouldn't believe and leaves you with a big, ugly bruise."

Molly and her team take a blood sample from the leatherback.

Turtle Tag

I

On a dark, wild beach in Tortuguero, Costa Rica, Molly Lutcavage tramped dejectedly over the black sand. It was four in the morning, pouring rain and Molly was tired, hungry and very discouraged. Ten days before, she and four other scientists had arrived at the sea turtle research station at Tortuguero to gather information on leatherbacks. Now their time was almost up. Molly had to return home to the United States later that day and so far she'd studied and tagged only two turtles.

Over the last 15 years she had often walked all night, up and down a nesting beach, and not found a single turtle. She knew by the way things were shaping up that this night would probably be the same. A flash of lightning in the sky rattled her nerves. Great. One more thing to worry about.

She had just about given up hope when the voice of one of the other scientists crackled over the radio in her hand. "We've found one!" crowed biologist Bill Jones. "You'd better hurry," piped in veterinarian Bob George, "she's nearly finished nesting!"

It takes a leatherback about an hour to dig a nest in the sand, lay anywhere from 60 to more than 100 eggs, fill in the cavity and start back to the sea. Molly knew that once the turtle picked up some speed, nothing would stop her from barrelling over the last short stretch of beach to the water. To reach the leatherback, Molly and sea turtle biologist Peter Bushnell and volunteer Charlie Blaney had about a kilometre to cover. They'd have to hustle if they were going to get there in time.

In the deep, leatherback lungs collapse, but they rely upon oxygen stores in their blood to keep them going.

There was no moon out that night and only a few stars. In the darkness, Molly and her two companions ran awkwardly down the beach. Among them, they were lugging about 14 kilograms (30 pounds) of equipment, including a bulky cargo net and tripod to weigh the turtle.

Even though she was an expert diver, it would be impossible for Molly to follow the leatherbacks under water. For one thing, she could stay below the surface without a tank only for about a minute. A leatherback dive might last anywhere from seven to 45 minutes, sometimes longer. And Molly's human lungs would collapse under the pressure of deep water. In the deep, leatherback lungs collapse, too, but they rely upon oxygen stores in their blood to keep them going. In fact, a leatherback can store more oxygen in its blood and tissues than it can in its lungs. "A sea turtle's lungs are different from other reptiles', " says Molly. "In a way, their lungs sort of resemble human lungs — they allow the turtles to very quickly exchange air (containing oxygen gas) in their bloodstreams. Sea turtles have evolved in such a way that they can spend most of their lives under water."

Leatherbacks are also the only reptile known to have the ability to stay warm in cold northern oceans and in the low temperatures of very deep water. Scientists call this special quality their "warm-bodiedness." Like many ocean creatures, leatherbacks have a fairly high **metabolism,** meaning they are able to convert the food they eat into energy at a pretty high rate. This helps them stay active (and warm) in cold water.

Molly knew leatherbacks could outswim her, too. "They're so fast, two strokes and they're gone, nobody can keep up with them." Leatherbacks can dive to depths of 1,000 metres (3,200 feet), maybe more, and clock a maximum diving speed of three metres (10 feet) a second.

> Leatherbacks are the only reptile known to have the ability to stay warm in cold northern oceans and in low temperatures of very deep water.

There was yet another problem: how do you find turtles in a wide, wide sea? The ocean is so vast and leatherbacks migrate farther than all other sea turtles, travelling between ice-cold Arctic waters and warm tropical seas. They have been traced as far north as Iceland and Alaska and as far south as the Cape of Good Hope. They are so rare and difficult to count that even Molly isn't sure how many leatherbacks are out on the high seas today. There may be 20,000 to 30,000 females, but because males don't come to shore it is almost impossible for scientists to estimate their numbers.

One place where leatherbacks tend to turn up is in the middle of fleets of jellyfish, their only food. Jellyfish are about 95 percent water — a very "energy poor" food. Molly calculated in one study that leatherbacks need to eat their own weight in jellyfish each day just to stay active and keep up their strength. The turtles also can be found on tropical beaches where they go every two or three years to lay their eggs.

Still, in spite of the challenges, Molly was fascinated by leatherbacks and amazed by their natural diving equipment. Since she couldn't dive with them, she'd used other ways to find out more about them. If she had to go on turtle patrol like other sea turtle biologists — up and down dark, rainy beaches — then that's what she did.

Panting and out of breath, Molly, Peter and Charlie arrived just in time. The leatherback had finished her egg-laying and was making great sweeps with her long fore-flippers, filling in the nest with sand. When she had covered the nest completely, the turtle turned back toward the sea. The scientists judged her direction and quickly spread a wide tarp over the sand. When the turtle had centred herself on the tarp, Molly and three other scientists each picked up a corner of the canvas and wrapped the leatherback in the tarp. Swaddled like a baby, with her flippers pressed against her sides, she couldn't hurt herself or the people around her.

The scientists hoisted the turtle with a big block and tackle and weighed her. She was 340 kilograms (750 pounds), an average size for an adult leatherback female. Molly inspected her soft, rubbery skin to check for tumours (none), barnacles (some) and scars from shark bites (none). She had a few marks on her neck where a mating male must have bitten her, but otherwise she was in good health and seemed unbothered by the remora that had attached itself to her back (a fish equipped with a big flat suction disk useful for attaching itself to larger animals for

If she had to go on turtle patrol like other sea turtle biologists—up and down dark, rainy beaches—then that's what she did.

ABOVE: *Her nest complete, the leatherback hauls herself back to the ocean.*

LEFT: *This leatherback lays her eggs by starlight.*

a free ride; remoras eat the detritus or floating leftovers, that their travelling host generates as it feeds). For future identification, Molly clipped a numbered metal tag to the turtle's right front flipper.

Now relaxed, the turtle needed to take only a couple of breaths each minute. The great force of sound she made with each breath blasted in the ears of the scientists as loudly as a whale's blow.

Molly's main purpose on that trip to Tortuguero was to gather leather-back blood samples from nesting females. With a **hypodermic** needle, she and Peter took several samples of the turtle's blood. Later they would examine them in their lab and confirm that leather-back blood has twice the oxygen-carrying capacity of any other sea turtles. It's no wonder they can dive so much deeper.

> For future identification, Molly clipped a numbered metal tag to the turtle's right front flipper.

When Molly had drawn the last sample, the leatherback was lowered gently to the ground and unwrapped. Free and rested after nearly 40 minutes in the cargo net, the turtle motored down the beach as fast as her powerful shoulders could drive her front flippers. Always so graceful in the water, she looked clumsy on land, but with a huge, hulking effort she pulled herself to the shore.

As dawn gave way to day, Molly stood in the light at the edge of the sea and watched a wave rise up and over the leatherback. As the wave drew back, another one came close behind and with it the turtle, the remora still attached to her back, was on her way. The turbid waters of Tortuguero were teaming with bull sharks, "full of life, but not the kind you'd want to swim with." Molly stopped short of envying the remora but she wished, as she had so many times before, that she could follow the leatherback.

Maybe one day, with the right gear, she will.

II

THE SCIENTIST:

Molly Lutcavage

When Molly was a kid growing up in a small mountain town in Pennsylvania, she never dreamed she'd one day find herself in a ratty T-shirt, a pair of old pants and her crummiest sneakers lugging heavy gear up and down a beach in the middle of the night looking for sea turtles. No way. In her dreams she had been wearing a really cool-looking wetsuit and diving to mysterious depths to explore the sea. "I actually never saw the ocean for real until I was 13 and my class went on a field trip to Atlantic City," she says. "But I was fascinated by the sea way before that. My favourite show on television was this underwater adventure program called *Sea Hunt*. It had all these scenes where the hero, Mike Nelson (actor Lloyd Bridges), battled bad guys under water and wrestled sharks ... I thought that was really exciting stuff!"

When Molly was 18 she had her first scuba-diving lesson. Right away she was hooked. "It was like going through a door to another world," she explains. It wasn't long after that she decided on her future — she was going to study diving animals.

"I always did well in science courses, but in 10th grade I had an eccentric college-prep biology teacher named Mary McNertney. Her demeanour was usually very stern, but she couldn't always hide her puckish sense of humour. I think she particularly enjoyed having kids like me in class, who were trying to do well because we liked biology, not because we wanted to get into medical school some day.

"In my junior year in college I took courses in invertebrate biology taught by

Hans Borei, a pipe-smoking Swedish professor. He used to sometimes say that women made good plankton counters and that was about it! But he said it on purpose, to get our goat and spur us to excel in the very male world of science." It worked. Molly bypassed a career in plankton-counting and went on to earn her master's, and Ph.D., and to eventually become a professor herself.

Molly got her master's degree in marine science from the Virginia Institute of Marine Science. When she was working on her thesis on the status of sea turtles in Chesapeake Bay and Virginia coastal waters, Virginia watermen (that's Virginian for "fishers") called her "Turtle Lady." Her thesis adviser had another name for her: Because Molly necropsied (examined post-mortem) so many dead, stranded sea turtles, he took to calling her "Molly Hatchet."

Molly earned her Ph.D. in biological oceanography from the Rosenstiel School of Marine and Atmospheric Sciences at the University of Miami. Her thesis was on gas exchange in the loggerhead sea turtle. Later, as a research scientist at the New England Aquarium's Edgerton Research Lab in Boston, Massachusetts, she studied sea turtles and giant bluefin tuna — another warmblooded deep diver. Today Molly is an associate research professor in the department of zoology at the University of New Hampshire.

"It was like going through a door to another world," she explains. It wasn't long after that she decided on her future — she was going to study diving animals.

Molly Lutcavage, associate research professor at the University of New Hampshire, with a satellite transmitter; one of the two types used to monitor leatherback turtles.

III THE SCIENCE:

High-tech Tagging

Knowing where leatherbacks go and when fishers can help avoid accidentally capturing the turtles in their longlines, gill nets or drift nets. "What we need to know is how many leatherbacks there are, and whether or not we are doing the right things to keep them safe and increase their numbers," says Molly. "When we take a conservation step, like protecting a nesting beach, if we don't have a benchmark number of how many turtles nested there to begin with, how can we know what's working?"

But getting this kind of information is not an easy task. Tag loss is often a problem for scientists and because leatherbacks can grow to such enormous sizes they seem to shed their tags at an even higher rate than other animals. If the tag is lost, so is all the data. "Nowadays, we often use PIT tags," says Molly. "PIT stands for passive information transponder. A PIT tag is actually a tiny little chip of information containing an identification number for future reference. The tag is so small it can be injected just under the leatherback's skin, behind its right shoulder, with a hypodermic needle. The scientists take advantage of the trance-like state the female is under while she lays her eggs to make the injection, which is so quick the turtle doesn't even seem to notice it happening. When scientists find a leatherback on a beach, they check for the PIT tag using a little machine that works using the same technology as the scanner at a grocery store checkout counter."

Another new tagging technology, satellite pop-up tags, holds great promise for leatherback and bluefin tuna research. To pop-up-tag a leatherback, scientists quickly drill a minuscule hole through the female turtle's **carapace** when she's on the beach to nest. They then anchor a tiny titanium screw under the carapace bone. The buoyant, egg-shaped tag is attached to a short titanium tether and floats just above the turtle's shoulder area. The buoyancy is vital: the tag contains a timer to self-release from the turtle and "pops up" to the ocean surface where its stores of data are transmitted to a satellite. The information is then directed to a data distribution service that deciphers it for Molly and her team.

The data that eventually arrive in Molly's e-mail in-basket record up to a year of sunrises and sunsets for use in geo-locating where tag and turtle were each day, temperature every hour and pressure readings to assess diving depths the turtle reached while under tag surveillance.

The information from female pop-up-tagged leatherbacks helps scientists identify their travel patterns. Unfortunately, there are drawbacks to the transmitters. Although the tags themselves don't harm the turtle, fish may bite through the tether connections or male leatherbacks wreck them when they clamp onto the female's back to mate.

> To pop-up-tag a leatherback, scientists quickly drill a minuscule hole through the female turtle's carapace when she's on the beach to nest.

THE ANIMAL NOTES:

Leatherback

128

Sea Turtle

Common name:	leatherback sea turtle	Family:	Dermochelyidae
Scientific name:	*Dermochelys coriacea*	Genus:	*Dermochelys*
Order:	Testudines	Species:	*coriacea*

Leatherbacks' staple food is jellyfish. Because jellyfish are 95 percent water, leatherbacks need to eat their own weight in jellyfish each day to stay active and keep up their strength.

Size/Weight:

Leatherbacks are the largest reptile in the world. Their shells can be as long as two metres (six-and-a-half feet) and the turtles regularly weigh 450 kilograms (1000 pounds).

Description:

Leatherbacks are the only sea turtles without a hard shell or scales. The leatherback's carapace (its upper "shell") is a series of bony plates and tough, oily connective tissue. It is bluish black with white blotches. The large front flippers are at least half as long as the carapace.

Reproduction:

Female leatherbacks dig a nest in the sand, lay from 60 to more than 100 eggs and bury them. It is the only time adult females return to land after hatching (males never return to land!). The baby turtles work sometimes for several days to dig out of their nest, erupting as a group.

Food:

Leatherbacks' staple food is jellyfish. Because jellyfish are 95 percent water, leatherbacks need to eat their own weight in jellyfish each day to stay active and keep up their strength.

Approximate lifespan:

Scientists are not sure how long it takes leatherback turtles to mature or how long they live.

Status:

Leatherbacks are so rare and difficult to count that scientists don't know how many there are. All seven species of sea turtles have suffered because of human activities:

construction of houses and resorts near a turtle-nesting beach may disturb the place so much that turtles won't return to lay more eggs; humans raid leatherback nests for eggs to eat or sell; the turtles can also starve to death if they mistake plastic-bag garbage in the oceans for jellyfish — once swallowed, the bags clog their guts and block their digestion; and leatherbacks can also get caught and drown in a fishing net. All this trouble makes a very poor picture for the future of leatherback sea turtles.

Habitat:

Because leatherbacks are difficult to study at sea, scientists do not know a lot about their best habitat. They do know that the leatherback has the largest geographic range of any reptile. It is also one of the deepest-diving air-breathing vertebrates, and can dive as far as one kilometre (just over half a mile) deep. Atlantic Canadian waters are popular in the summer because there are a lot of jellyfish.

Range/distribution:

Leatherbacks are found in the Atlantic, Pacific and Indian oceans. They migrate from as far north as Iceland and Alaska to as far south as the Cape of Good Hope.

At ten paces, Bruce stopped, raised the gun and shot a tranquilizer dart on target into Blanche's rump.

Bruce takes down the snare that holds a grizzly to the tree.

Bruce and Blanche

Blanche the grizzly was one smart bear. She wasn't tricky like Pete, who had so many different ways of springing snares to steal bait that the biologists he foiled nicknamed him "the infamous professor." But she never got caught goofing around, either. Not like Elizabeth, who was spotted one April morning digging a deep hole in snow, sticking her head in and tipping upside down to stand on her shoulders. In this pose she rocked back and forth, wiggling her legs at the sky, until she fell over and had to start again.

Biologist Bruce McLellan and his wife, Celine, first saw Blanche on October 10, 1979, out in front of their little cabin in British Columbia's remote Flathead River valley. Unsettled by people, the surrounding mountains, meadows and gravelly river basin made for prime grizzly country. In spring where the snow melted early, bears could find roots of hedysarum and green grasses. In the mountains they'd find white bark and peel off strips to gnaw at the sugary layer underneath the bark. They might come upon a thawed carcass of a mountain goat or bring down a weak old deer starved by winter. In summer, nature added horsetails, sedges, blueberries, huckleberries and mountain ash berries to the menu. By autumn, the ground squirrels were fat enough to fill the maw of any lucky bear that plowed into their burrows. Come the first signs of winter, when food would be hard to find, dens could be dug into the mountainside or under a tangle of tree roots in the subalpine forest and the grizzlies would retire to hibernate until spring.

> **"A bear's whole world goes through its nose," says Bruce. "They use their sense of smell the way humans rely on sight and sound."**

Yes, the Flathead was a very good place to study grizzlies. At the time Bruce lived there he estimated there were about 100 grizzlies in the region. Still, it wasn't every day that a mother grizzly and her three cubs came into his front yard.

"A bear's whole world goes through its nose," says Bruce. "They use their sense of smell the way humans rely on sight and sound. By smell, bears know who's around and what happened there yesterday." The bears themselves, says Bruce, smell "sort of like a dog." That day, these bears' noses were drawn to Bruce's truck. It smelled of meat transported as bait for the foot-snare Bruce used to catch bears for a brief examination. The truck was empty, but in the time it took the bears to figure that out, Bruce sneaked out of the cabin, quickly baited a snare with a chunk of rotten butcher cuttings and anchored it to a tree at the edge of the yard.

Bruce knew that if the bears sensed humans in the area they might leave before the big female found the bait. So as soon as the bears ambled away from the truck, Bruce and Celine got in and drove off to leave the family alone for a while.

They returned at dark and found the mother grizzly, huffing and struggling, her right front foot caught in the snare. Two of the cubs were up the tree; the third was hiding further back in the woods.

By now the sun had disappeared behind the trees and it was too dark to work safely. Bruce and Celine went back to the cabin and listened until at last the mother bear settled down for the night.

At first light the McLellans returned with a name for the bear — Blanche — and a specially designed dart gun. At 10 paces, Bruce stopped, raised the gun and shot a tranquilizer dart on target into Blanche's rump. She was immobilized in five minutes.

The first thing Bruce did was release her foot from the snare. He snapped permanent metal tags, one in each ear (in case one fell off), with the number 385 engraved on both of them. Then he weighed her. With ropes tied around her wrists and ankles, Blanche was hoisted about two-and-a-half centimetres (about an inch) off the ground with a long pole. She tipped the scales at 129.25 kilograms (285 pounds). After setting her gently down and removing the ropes, Bruce extended his measuring tape from Blanche's nose to her tail and wrote "1.73 metres" (68 inches) on her record. Lifting her head, Bruce checked her teeth and pulled a very tiny premolar (smaller than a human baby tooth) from her gum. A bear adds a new layer to its teeth every year. This tooth had 15 layers, meaning Blanche was a 15-year-old grizzly. Finally, he fastened a radio collar around her neck and then left her alone to wake up a few hours later.

Blanche got to her feet groggily and ambled off to join her cubs, who had been watching anxiously from the other side of the river. Reunited, mother and cubs disappeared into the cottonwoods that lined the riverbank.

Scientists think that, just like human fingerprints, each grizzly's set of broad-footed paws is unique. Individual bears also have different characters; some are more intelligent, serious, aggressive, curious or shy than others. From then on, Bruce tracked Blanche almost every field day. By watching her closely over time, he learned what else made her different.

In the next six years Blanche had two more litters of triplets. Bruce says she was a good mother to all of them, a serious bear with not much time for goofing around. When foraging, "Blanche was quite a sampler. She would hit eight or nine berry patches in the summer and then stay in the best one." She really liked buffalo berries, which Bruce says is a little strange: bears do eat them, but as far as he's concerned they "taste really crappy."

Blanche's range was interesting. She stayed in the valleys and rarely went into the mountains like many other grizzlies in the Flathead. Depending on where they

This tooth had 15 layers, meaning Blanche was a 15-year-old grizzly.

ABOVE: *The state of a bear's teeth is a valuable indicator of its health and age.*

LEFT: *Bruce measures a tranquilized grizzly. The cloth protects the bear's eyes from insects, dirt and sunlight.*

live and how abundant food is in their habitat, a female grizzly's range might be 20 to 400 square kilometres (eight to 150 square miles), a male's as vast as 5,000 square kilometres (1,900 square miles). Blanche had a 320-square-kilometre (125-square-mile) range.

As omnivores, grizzly bears eat a variety of plant foods and meat. Depending on what's available at the time, a grizzly's diet might be up to 90 percent plants. The bears have strong memories of good places to feed and they will return to them every year. They also remember bad experiences and places to avoid. Bruce and Celine have tagged 130 grizzlies in the 20 years they've lived and worked in the Flathead, and none of the six they found in the yard ever came back for a second go. After that day in the yard, Bruce managed to trap Blanche and check on her only two more times. She had learned to avoid anything that smelled like that pesky biologist.

> She had learned to avoid anything that smelled like that pesky biologist.

On his 33rd birthday, October 25, 1986, Bruce was walking home from the British Columbia-Montana border when a man in a truck drove up to him and got out. "There's a road-killed elk and a dead bear near the side of the road, up there," the man told Bruce and gave him the number he'd seen on the bear's ear tag — 385.

By then Bruce had tagged hundreds and hundreds of black and grizzly bears and had 385 been any other bear he would have had to check his records for the name. But he knew who 385 was. With a heavy heart he walked the rest of the way to his truck and drove up the road to find out what had happened.

He stopped when he saw the elk. Blanche must have been feeding on it when she was killed. Following a trail of blood a little way into the woods, he found Blanche. His eyes blurred and his throat tightened as he bent down to examine her. She'd put on some weight since the day he'd first met her, another 20 kilograms (44 pounds), and her fur was darker. Bruce stroked through Blanche's bloodied fur and found the place where the bullet had entered her heart. Then he stood up and began to examine the scene around him.

The kill was illegal — grizzly hunting was allowed in the Flathead only in spring. Grizzlies and black bears are sometimes killed illegally for their parts, claws are made into jewellery, hides and heads are taken as trophies and other parts are used in some traditional Asian medicines. An increasing number of people and roads that provide easy access to grizzly country is a big concern for bear biologists like Bruce. Roads don't kill grizzlies, but they bring people carrying guns who do. But Blanche's body had not been touched.

Conservation officers came, investigated and dragged Blanche deep into the woods. A week later Bruce went back to where they had left her but he couldn't find a trace of the old bear anywhere. Like the person who killed her, Blanche's carcass was never found.

Blanche had three cubs with her when she died: Bert, Ernie and a third that was never identified. Ernie was shot by a hunter in the Flathead, in a place near his mother's range, when he was nine. And Bert? He made his way down to Montana. His collar came off around 1988 and biologists haven't had sign of him since.

One of Blanche's daughters from the trio that trooped into the McLellan yard 19 years ago still roams the Flathead. Shy, hard to catch and clever enough to stretch out a cable's snares to steal all the bait inside, Bruce calls her "Aggie" and he smiles when he says she's "really smart — just like her mother."

II THE SCIENTIST:
Bruce McLellan

Bruce McLellan was four years old when he saw his first grizzly. It was 1958. The McLellan family was living in Lake Louise in the Rocky Mountains, where Bruce's father, an engineer, was designing a ski lift.

"It was a summer morning, about dawn. My mother woke us up and ushered us to the living room window. Our house overlooked the Pipestone River and we saw a young grizzly, not very big, snuffling about on the far side. Bruce wasn't afraid of the bear, just interested. Really interested. At the same time, a herd of elk was browsing in the backyard. With a bear on one side and elk on the other, the house was pretty much surrounded. Bruce's dad was late for work that day, because he had to wait until the coast was clear before heading out the door.

Bruce didn't begin his career as a bear guy and it even took a while before he settled on biology as a career. After high school he worked on ski hills, ranches, with logging crews and as a carpenter before turning to biology. His first stints in the field were studies of elk and mountain goats. Large carnivores held for him a special fascination that he finds hard to explain. "For people who are fascinated with large carnivores, it's instinctive," he says simply.

It's not just about the animals for Bruce, it's the whole way of life. "I've always been really attracted to wild places and my work has taken me to them all over the world." He says all the trappings of wildlife biology and fieldwork suit his character — he can put up with mosquitoes and give up the comforts of modern cities gladly for a chance to live and work in nature. "I like to fetch my own water," he says. "I like going down to the river with a pail in my hand. There's so much to see."

"I've always been really attracted to wild places and my work has taken me to them all over the world."

Bruce McLellan, shown here with two young grizzly cubs, is senior wildlife habitat ecologist for the British Columbia Ministry of Forests in Revelstoke, B.C.

III

THE SCIENCE:

Tracking Bear Habits

For decades, biologists have been searching for gentler ways to identify bears. In the meantime they try to bother them at close range only for an hour or two and only every couple of years.

There's no getting around it: trapping is frightening for bears and sometimes they hurt themselves when struggling to be free of the snare. But if scientists are going to learn what a bear needs and does to survive, and to record individual characteristics, the best way is still to tranquilize, tag and describe the animal in their log.

Before capture and live-release techniques took hold, early naturalists did a lot of observing and collecting to study wildlife. Their research tools amounted to little more than a notebook, a pair of binoculars and a rifle. Bears were just one of many species shot for study and mounted for museum displays.

By the late 1950s, capture, marking and live release of bears had replaced specimen-collecting in North America. Bears in Yellowstone National Park were among the first to be fitted with radio collars in the early 1960s. Radio collars have since become "the backbone" of bear and large mammal research.

To help scientists map bear movements and ranges, some bears are now collared with global positioning systems (GPS) that pick up on satellite signals and are programmed to transmit a bear's location data every five or six hours. They could record a location as frequently as every hour, but Bruce says that's hard on the battery, and replacing a GPS collar frequently means bugging the bear more often, which is what scientists try to avoid in the first place.

GPS collars have their limits: they are expensive, and they don't function well from forests. Another technique used to track bear movement and habitat patterns that is gaining ground is DNA research. A small sack of rotting meat, or a douse of old fish oil —"something that stinks"— is used to draw a bear to an area where some barbed wire has been set at bear level to catch a bit of hair. A couple of strands of bear hair with roots is all scientists need for a laboratory DNA test that will identify the individual, the species and sex. Collect enough of these samples, compile the data and patterns of habitat use, and movement over vast areas begins to emerge. DNA analysis is also helpful in understanding the genetic exchange that keeps bear populations healthy. "And we don't even have to catch the bears to do it," says Bruce. "It doesn't bother them at all, except maybe they're disappointed the smell they were following didn't turn out to be a meal."

> DNA analysis is also helpful in understanding the genetic exchange that keeps bear populations healthy.

Tranquilizing and trapping techniques have changed over the years to be more "bear friendly." Today, Bruce uses a tranquilizer dart fastened to the end of a ski pole. It takes about five minutes for the injection to take effect and as soon as it does the bear is unsnared and the examination quickly completed.

The newer drugs wear off more quickly, too. Twenty-five years ago, the sedative effect of a bear tranquilizer lingered and groggy bears were more vulnerable to an opportunistic hunter or another bear.

IV

THE ANIMAL NOTES:

Grizzly

Bear

Common name:	grizzly bear	Family:	Ursidae
Scientific name:	*Ursus arctos horribilis*	Genus:	*Ursus*
		Species:	*arctos*
Order:	Carnivora	Subspecies:	*horribilis*

Their future as a species now depends upon the healthy populations that remain in parts of British Columbia, the Yukon, Alaska and Russia.

Size/Weight:

At birth, grizzly bear cubs weigh about one kilogram (2 pounds). An average weight for a 12- to 18-year-old male grizzly is about 227 kilograms (500 pounds); a female about half that.

Description:

Grizzly bears are usually darkish brown but can vary from very light cream to black. As they age, the ends of their hair can develop silvery-grey tips, giving them a "grizzled" appearance. The grizzly has a large hump over the shoulders and extremely long front claws.

Reproduction:

Of all North America's large carnivores, grizzlies reproduce most slowly. On average, a female grizzly will have cubs only every three or four years. Generally, the richer the habitat, the more cubs a female may have. Because grizzly bears reproduce so slowly, in some areas even the killing of one or two females each year can jeopardize a population.

Food:

Grizzly bears are omnivores. They will prey on mammals and migrating salmon, when available, but their diet can be up to 90 percent plants.

Approximate lifespan:

Bears in the wild live up to 25 years. Counting the number of layers in the cement holding a bear's tooth in the socket will tell its age — one layer for each year of the grizzly's life.

Status:

A thousand years ago, grizzly bears (or "brown bears" as they are commonly called) could be found in North America, Asia, the Middle East, Europe, Great Britain and even northern Africa. In the mid-1800s there might have been as many as 100,000 grizzlies in the lower 48 United States alone. Today they are listed as a threatened species in the lower 48 United States under the Endangered Species Act. Canada has about 20,000 to 25,000 grizzlies remaining in British Columbia, Alberta, the Northwest Territories and the Yukon. Their future as a species now depends upon the healthy populations that remain in parts of British Columbia, the Yukon, Alaska and Russia.

Habitat:

All the varied habitats a grizzly needs to survive are like a multitextured patchwork quilt over the course of a year: river valleys for foraging; mountain slopes for berries; alpine meadows for burrowing marmots; forested valleys for naps, high mountain caves for winter dens ... This variety in a grizzly bear's range may extend anywhere from 70 square kilometres to well over 1,000, depending upon the abundance of available food sources.

Range:

Grizzly bears are found in North America, eastern and western Europe, northern Asia and in Japan. In North America, grizzlies are found in western Canada, Alaska, and in the states of Wyoming, Montana, Idaho and Washington. Grizzlies have the widest distribution of any bear species

Biologist and wolf stood there and studied each other as the snow fell and the wind began to howl.

In North America, the basic colours of the grey wolf are grey, black and white, although they may also sport cream, buff, tawny, reddish, or blue-black coats.

Finding Phyllis

It was the perfect house for a Viking. A two-storey log cabin, set in the middle of a meadow nearly a kilometre (half a mile) long, enough to land a small airplane. Built in 1909, every year the spaces between its logs let in more of the Montana winter than they kept out. No matter how many rags and newspapers were used to fill the cracks, winter always made its way inside with icy determination, along with the occasional weasel, pack rat or chipmunk. There was no electricity. No indoor plumbing. No neighbours close by.

A Viking would have loved it. Vikings and cold just go together. Not that a Viking lived there in the 1980s, but Diane Boyd did.

Close enough.

If you asked Diane, she would confess to merely tolerating summer, with its heat and bugs. Like the Vikings of old, it is winter she loves. And Montana winters, during which temperatures can drop 30 or 40 degrees Celsius below zero (minus 22 to minus 40 degrees Fahrenheit), do not disappoint.

It was into the snow-covered clearing surrounding Diane's cabin in northern Montana, on the border of Glacier National Park, that one clear morning in March 1988, wolf number 8550 stepped out of the forest and into her sight. Diane had just emerged from the outhouse and was heading back to the cabin when she saw 8550 —"Phyllis"— standing at the forest edge, looking straight back at her.

Even at a kilometre (half a mile) away, with snow falling around them, Diane recognized Phyllis immediately. Her colour always gave her away. Rare as wolves were in Montana (and in 1988 there were only about 20), Phyllis was rarer still — she is the only white wolf Diane has ever seen in the West.

South of the Canadian Arctic, the gene pool is pretty shallow for white wolves — less than 2 percent of wolves in the south are white. This may explain why a young, healthy, pure white wolf like Phyllis was such an unusual sight in the Rockies.

Biologist and wolf stood there and studied each other as the snow fell and the wind began to howl. It was Phyllis who broke the spell when she turned and disappeared back into the forest. Diane raced to the cabin for her skis and followed Phyllis' tracks for a few kilometres (a couple of miles), until she ran out of daylight. There was no hope of catching up to her because wolves can easily travel 48 kilometres (30 miles) per day. As for following her the next day, no hope again. By morning, new-fallen snow had erased every track.

In 1982, a grey wolf numbered 114 and named Kishinena bore a litter of pups in southern British Columbia, in a part of the Rockies barely a cat's spring from Glacier National Park. Diane was in Montana to study the natural return of wolves to the Rocky Mountains of the western United States, from which they had been **extirpated** by the late 1930s through rigorous hunting, poisoning and trapping.

Kishinena's territory included the North Fork of the Flathead River and overlapped Diane's study area, and it was one of Kishinena's offspring that crossed the invisible border from Canada to the United States and played a key role in re-establishing *Canis lupus* south of the 49th parallel. That wolf, who walked down on her own into the United States and Glacier National Park, was young Phyllis.

Phyllis' white colour made her easily recognizable, but she was all the more memorable in wolf research for her intelligence and elusiveness.

And could she ever be elusive. In fact, it took a grizzly bear snare to catch Phyllis off guard. One of Diane's nearest neighbours was Canadian grizzly bear biologist Bruce McLellan (see chapter 9). It was Bruce who found the two-year-old Phyllis in a research snare he'd set for a bear one day in May 1985. Although it happens sometimes that the wrong animal gets into the wrong trap — (Diane has even caught bears in wolf snares) "things that are big tend to pull out" so it wasn't as if Bruce carried wolf-size radio collars just in case.

> Phyllis' white colour made her easily recognizable, but she was all the more memorable in wolf research for her intelligence and elusiveness.

Fortunately, Diane says, "wolf people and bear people help each other out." Diane was out tracking wolves the morning Phyllis was caught, so Bruce headed down to her cabin, found a wolf radio collar and tranquilized Phyllis long enough that he could put it on her. He gave her a good checking over, assessed her to be at least two, possibly three years old, based on the condition of her teeth and noted that she was **lactating** — she had pups somewhere. Unfortunately, Bruce had to release Phyllis before Diane could be reached.

Diane was sorry she'd missed the chance to study Phyllis close up but she was grateful to have her "on the air" with her radio collar. "Phyllis was a very important wolf," says Diane. Over a long period of time, a profile of Phyllis began to emerge, proving just how important she was.

In April 1986, the year after she was collared, Phyllis denned in Glacier and bore a litter of five grey pups. Some scientists dubbed her new family the "Magic Pack," because it was the first time a wolf had denned in Glacier, or anywhere else in Montana for that matter, in more than half a century.

In 1987, Phyllis separated from her pack. She headed to the northern portion of the pack's range, back into Canada, where she denned and gave birth to her last litter of pups in May, about a month later than usual. Because wolves generally follow the same denning times year after year, Phyllis' delay made for a remarkable finding during the course of Diane's research. For one thing, wolves don't get pregnant at just any time in the year. There are only a few short weeks every year during which their bodies come into heat to prepare for pupping. That a female wolf could delay that period until a mate was available was a new discovery in wolf biology. Diane believes it's possible that Phyllis, as a lone wolf, deliberately scent-marked (with her scat and urine) to advertise her new address to a male wolf and that it just took her a little longer to attract a mate than if she'd paired up with a pack's alpha male. But if Phyllis wasn't scent-marking along her travel routes and leaving scat where other wolves would find it, how else could she have attracted a mate?

By the end of 1988, Phyllis was no longer alone as she had been the first time Diane saw her. She had her pups, and some of the members of the Magic Pack had

It was the first time a wolf had denned
in Glacier, or anywhere else in
Montana for that matter, in more
than half a century.

ABOVE: *A single pack of wolves may contain animals that are many shades of grey.*

LEFT: *When Phyllis headed back into the forest, she left a trail of tracks. But they
would only last until the next snowfall.*

come to join her in British Columbia. Phyllis roamed the Flathead Valley until 1989, but never had another litter. The pack disintegrated completely in another year and for a time Phyllis travelled with her one surviving pup, until that wolf, too, disappeared and Phyllis was alone.

Meanwhile, Diane did everything she could to try to catch her again to replace her radio collar before it failed. Trap placement is a science in itself. Diane had to set traps along wolf travel routes and their scent-mark stops. They could not be too close to a river or stream, or a panicked wolf might drag itself into the water and possibly drown before the scientists could arrive. And they couldn't be so far up a hill that a wolf could tumble down and dislocate a leg trying to get free. Nor could there be logs, stumps or rocks in the area to entangle a trapped wolf. To fully conceal the traps, Diane buried them in the ground. They were hair-trigger sensitive and even the lightest touch would snap them shut.

Wolves cannot be fooled by bait; a wolf trap must be totally scentless and hidden. Without a bait reward, it is just a piece of steel hidden in the ground. You'd think

Phyllis would have left the traps alone and maybe she ignored a few, but Diane lost count of all the traps Phyllis dug out and left exposed, most of them unsnapped.

For all Diane's efforts, Phyllis was never caught again. The collar Bruce put on her went dead near the end of 1988. After that, Diane believed she was still living somewhere in the Flathead Valley but that was all she knew for a long time.

Phyllis had been off the air for a year or two when word came to Diane from friends in southwestern Alberta that a white wolf wearing a black collar had been spotted hanging around a remote work camp. The men fed her scraps and she became friendly with the camp's two dogs. Sometimes she slept under one of the cabins. The men could see she was past her prime; arthritis had probably set in and her teeth would have been well worn down. An aging, lone wolf, Phyllis had traded some of her wariness of humans for camp scraps to supplement her meagre hunting.

The average lifespan of a wolf in the wild is three or four years. Even a six- or seven-year-old wolf is pretty unusual. Phyllis made it past her 10th birthday.

She was shot in Alberta on December 19, 1992, by a hunter with a legal permit. Had she been in the United States she might have lived longer, as the wolf is protected in the lower 48 states by the Endangered Species Act. But wolves don't recognize the political or park boundaries that prohibit hunting. In Canada wolves are a legal game animal, because Canada is home to one of the world's last relatively healthy populations of wolves.

The hunter had nothing to hide. He submitted Phyllis' radio collar when he reported the kill to Canadian officials. The collar information was returned to the University of Montana, the sponsor of Diane's study, and they got in touch with her immediately. Because it was Phyllis, Diane drove up to Alberta. She met the hunter and talked to him for a long time. She never saw Phyllis' body — it was being mounted by a taxidermist. But the hunter told her Phyllis had seemed to be in good shape, at least not starving, when she died. And he, too, marvelled over the rare beauty of her white coat. This hunter was very proud of having her; he didn't shoot her out of malice.

Diane told the hunter a little more about Phyllis and he learned that more than her coat made her special. She told him Phyllis gave birth to her first litter of seven pups in 1985 in British Columbia. She said that along with her 1986 litter of five, and another litter of six born in 1987, Phyllis was the mother of a total of 18 pups, some of whom survived, rose to alpha status (in wolf society it is only the leaders of the pack, the alpha male and the alpha female, who mate) and reared pups of their own in Montana. History would one day remember Phyllis as the mother, and Kishinena the grandmother, of the return of wolves to the northwestern United States.

The cabin where Diane lived is gone now, swept away by a flood in 1995. Phyllis' offspring are also long gone, and her bloodline has mixed so far into the wolves of the Rockies as to be untraceable — the way snow covers wolf tracks, as if they had never been. Snow keeps stories only for so long, but science records them forever. Because of Diane's research, number 8550, the white wolf of the West, and mother of Montana's first litter of wolves in more than 50 years, is going to be remembered for a long, long time to come.

II THE SCIENTIST:

Diane Boyd

Despite an ability to team up to bring down big game, a wolf's life is feast or famine — and most of the time it's famine. "They're basically programmed for starvation," says Diane. In this way, wolves have something in common with the "lean and hungry" grad students Diane supervised during the Wolf Ecology Project, which ran from 1979 to 1993. Diane earned her master's degree in wildlife biology in 1982 from the University of Montana and in 1997 the university awarded her a Ph.D. in fish and wildlife biology. Much of her 25-year career has been spent studying wolves in remote parts of Montana and Canada. But the wolf, formerly one of the most widespread species in the world, also has drawn Diane to work with wolves in the Northwest Territories, Minnesota, Michigan, Arizona, New Mexico, Romania and Italy. Dr. Diane Boyd also served as the executive director of the Teller Wildlife Refuge in Corvallis, Montana.

> **Despite an ability to team up to bring down big game, a wolf's life is feast or famine — and most of the time it's famine.**

At the time of this story, Diane was a research specialist with the University of Montana. For 15 years she lived in a meadow with no name in a remote part of Montana near Glacier National Park where she pioneered research on wolf recolonization in the central Rocky Mountains.

For 15 years she lived in a meadow with no name in a remote part of Montana near Glacier National Park.

Diane Boyd attaches a tracking collar to a tranquilized wolf.

THE SCIENCE:

The Season of the Wolf

No job posting for a wolf biologist ever says "must love winter," but it helps. After all, winter is the season of the wolf. It is the time to follow tracks in snow, to inspect perfectly preserved frozen scat and to count icy dribbled patterns of urine, the wolf's primary scent-marking device. Hard-crusted snow makes the perfect platter for the remains of a deer carcass, abandoned by wolves to await the inspection of a biologist who can swiftly ski or snowshoe to the site rather than slog through muddy, rocky, tangled terrain. Winter preserves, between snowfalls, many stories for scientists to read in the snow; among them the tracks of the chase by wolves as they hunt down prey.

Snow gives wolves the advantage. Their wide feet are perfectly designed for running on snow and ice.

Snow gives wolves the advantage. Their wide feet are perfectly designed for running on snow and ice whereas ungulates, the hooved mammals — deer, moose, and elk — that make up a wolf pack's primary prey, are not. Crusty conditions make travel difficult for ungulates: their weight, balanced on four sharp hooves, punches through the snow crust and their long legs sink, slowing their movements to a struggle. But most of the time the prey escapes the wolves, who have a hunting success average of approximately five percent.

In analyzing data on wolf-killed white-tailed deer and elk in Glacier National Park during her study, Diane was able to confirm the importance not only of deep snow but also of the thickness of the snow's crust to the hunting success of a wolf pack. In her studies, snow depth of about 50 centimetres (20 inches) or more begins to slow down deer. If snow were a pizza, wolves would order up deep-dish and thin crust every time.

While it's often said that wolves cull the weak, the sick, the old and the very young from populations, Diane cautions that this is not the full story. Environmental conditions like deep, thinly crusted snow can instantly turn a strong, healthy moose (capable of killing a wolf with one swift kick to the cranium) into a vulnerable mass of potential protein. In a world with so much against them, where a history of persecution by hunting, trapping and poisoning has brought wolves to the brink of extinction in many parts of their former range, it's a good thing they still have winter on their side.

THE ANIMAL NOTES:

Grey

Wolf

Common name:	grey wolf	Family:	Canidae
	Also known as timber wolf	Genus:	*Canis*
Scientific name:	*Canis lupus*	Species:	*lupus*
Order:	Carnivora		

Their future as a species now depends upon the healthy populations that remain in parts of British Columbia, the Yukon, Alaska and Russia.

Size/Weight:

Males can weigh from 30 to 80 kilograms (65 to 175 pounds), with an average of 55 kilos (120 pounds); females can weigh from 23 to 55 kilos (50 to 120 pounds), with an average of 45 kilos (100 pounds). Height, measured from base of paws to shoulder, generally ranges from 60 to 90 centimetres (23 to 35 inches).

Description:

Wolves have a very large head compared with their body size, long legs, large paws and obvious facial markings. Their basic colours are grey, black and white, although grey wolves can also have cream, buff, reddish or blue black coats. A single pack may contain animals that are many shades. Wether grey, black or tawny, North American wolves may also morph colours if they live long enough. Like humans, wolves tend to grey as they age.

Reproduction:

Both male and female wolves in the wild can breed only once a year. Most litters are born in April; after a nine-week gestation period, litters of five or six pups (though sometimes eight or more) are born.

Food:

Ungulates (hooved mammals such as moose, deer and elk) make up the primary prey. Wolves also eat a variety of smaller mammals and birds, but these form only a small part of their diet.

Approximate Lifespan:

The average lifespan of a wolf in the wild is three or four years.

Status:

Two hundred years ago, grey wolves were more widely distributed than any other mammal of historic times. Today, Canada is home to one of the world's last relatively healthy population of wolves. In the United States, wolves are protected by

Habitat:

Grey wolves are one of the most wide-ranging land animals. They occupy a broad variety of habitats, from Arctic tundra to forest, Prairie and arid landscapes.

Range/distribution:

Originally, the grey wolf ranged over most of the Northern Hemisphere, including northern Africa and southern Asia. However, due to habitat destruction, environmental change and persecution by humans, grey wolf populations are now found only in a few areas of the contiguous United States, Alaska, Canada, Mexico (a small population) and Eurasia.

Acknowledgements

There comes a point in every book's progress to print that the metabolic momentum to fuel it forward must be drawn not from the author, but from new sources. When the manuscript for *Wild Science* left my computer it went first to my agent, then the good people at Raincoast, eventually to design and proofs and print. At each stage, a new contribution was made, until we had something whole and complete and unlike anything any of us could find anywhere. So my thanks are to these people, who, in turn and in tandem, made this book what it is. To David Nunuk, not only for the picture, but for saying the simplest, best thing anyone could say to an author, right when she needed to hear it most. And meaning it. To designer Gabi Proctor, who's gifted artistic vision gave these stories the look they so deserved. To my editor, Simone Doust, who championed this project from the day it landed on her desk. Simone's sheer hard work and rare skill brought my manuscript to life in a book with more dimensions than I'd ever dreamed of. To my agent, Elizabeth Harding, for knowing exactly where *Wild Science* belonged and working so diligently through the process to bring it on home. And to Jon, Andrew, Ian, Marianne, Quinton, Janet, Kathleen, Molly, Bruce, Amy, Minga and Diane for sharing their stories, answering all my dumb questions and patiently working through the text in all its evolutions. I think you're all as extraordinary as the animals you work with and it is my great privilege to say so in print.

164

Picture credits

Glossary

carapace: A turtle's shell

cetaceans: Any marine mammal of the order Cetacea, characterized by a streamlined, hairless body and a dorsal blowhole for breathing. including whales, dolphins, and porpoises.

dander: Loose skin-scales shed from an animal's coat or feathers.

echolocation: Determining the location of objects by reflected sound (see pages 94-95).

extirpate: To make an animal extinct in a certain part of its range.

forage: The act of searching for food.

frond: The leaf or leaf-like part of a palm fern or similar plant.

gillnetters: Fishers who use a net that catches fish by their gills

grapnel: A small anchor with several claws.

guano: Seabird or bat excrement (poop).

hibernacula: The shelter of hibernating animals.

holdfast: The organ that anchors an aquatic plant to something solid, often a rock or boulder, on the substrate.

hypodermic: An injection under the skin.

krill: Small, shrimp-like crustaceans.

lactating: Secreting (producing and releasing) milk.

metabolic rate (metabolism): The sum total of chemical reactions that result in energy production and maintain the life of a living thing.

parasites: Organisms which live on, and takes nutrients from, another plant or animal.

pectoral: Of or relating to the breast or chest. On fish, pectoral fins are based one on either side behind the head, in corresponding position to the arms or forelegs of higher vertebrates (animals with backbones).

prehensile: Capable of grasping.

primates: Any animal of the order Primates, the highest order of mammals, including lemurs, tarsiers, monkeys, apes and human beings.

telemetry: The science and technology of automatic measurement and transmission of data by wire, radio, or other means from remote sources to receiving stations for recording and analysis. Satellites transmit their data by telemetry.

Resources

Canadian Wildlife Service - www.cws-scf.ec.gc.ca

World Wildlife Fund – www.panda.org

Memorial University Whale Research Group, Memorial University of Newfoundland, St. John's, Newfoundland

Marmot Recovery Foundation, Nanaimo, British Columbia - www.marmots.org

Monterey Bay Aquarium, Monterey, California - www.montereybayaquarium.com

Jacksonville University Manatee Research Project, Jacksonville, Florida - www.ju.edu/academics/research_marco_research_growth.asp

Bat Conservation International, Austin, Texas - www.batcon.org

Teller Wildlife Refuge (Corvallis, Montana) - www.tellerwildlife.org

BOOKS

America's Neighborhood Bats, Merlin D. Tuttle (University of Texas Press, 1988)

The Adventures of Phokey the Sea Otter: Based on a True Story, Marianne Riedman (Sequoyah Publishing, 1996)

The Polar Bear, Ian Stirling (University of Michigan Press, 1988)

Sea Otters, Marianne Riedman (Monterey Bay Aquarium Foundation, 1990)

Stelleluna, Janelle Cannon (Harcourt, 1999)

Silverwing, Kenneth Oppel (Harper Collins, 1998)

Wet and Fat: Whales and Seals of Newfoundland and Labrador, Jon Lien (Breakwater Books, 1985)

Index